Nana Awere Damoah was born in Accra, Ghana. He holds a Masters degree in Chemical Engineering from the University of Nottingham, UK, and a Bachelors in Chemical Engineering from the Kwame Nkrumah University of Science and Technology (KNUST), Kumasi, Ghana. Nana spent all his secondary or high school years at Ghana National College, Cape Coast, Ghana and speaks fondly of growing up in the suburb of Kotobabi in the Ghanaian capital, where he started his education at the local Providence Preparatory School.

A British Council Chevening alumnus, Nana works with Unilever West Africa. He is an associate of Joyful Way Incorporated, a Christian Music Ministry in Ghana, where he was the group's National President from 2002 to 2004. Nana now serves on Joyful Way's Board.

Nana started writing seriously in 1993 when he was in the sixth form and has had a number of his short stories published in the *Mirror* and the *Spectator* newspapers. In 1997, he won first prize in the Step Magazine National Story Writing Competition. His writing has appeared in StoryTime ezine, Legon Business Journal, Sentinel Nigeria Magazine and the anthology African Roar (StoryTime Publishing, 2010).

He is the author of two non-fiction books: Through the Gates of Thought (2010) and Excursions in my Mind (2008). He keeps a personal blog at www.nanadamoah.com, is the creator and editor of StoryLoom and Ghanamanisms (www.storyloom.wordpress.com and www.ghanamanisms.wordpress.com, dedicated to Ghanaian fiction and non-fiction, respectively) and is a columnist of *Business and Financial Times* newspaper.

He is married to Vivian. The couple and their children, Nana Kwame Bassanyin, Nana Yaw Appiah, and Maame Esi Akoah, are based in Tema, Ghana.

TALES FROM DIFFERENT TAILS

TALES
FROM DIFFERENT
TAILS

NANA AWERE DAMOAH

TALES FROM DIFFERENT TAILS

ISBN 978-1-47006-768-7

Cover Design and Book Layout by multiPIXEL Limited
P O Box Dc1965, Dansoman, Accra, Ghana.
Email: multipixellimited@gmail.com
Tel: + 233 302 333 502 | +233 246 725 060 | +233 246 201 862

Illustrations by John Benjamin Yanney (multiPIXEL Limited)

Author's Contact: Nana A. Damoah
Email: ndamoah@yahoo.co.uk

Dedicated to Scripture Union, Burning Fire, Joyful Way Incorporated, Literary Wing of the Inter-hall Christian Fellowship (IHCF) of the Kwame Nkrumah University of Science and Technology and the Graduate Christian Fellowship (GCF) of University of Nottingham – groups that shaped my writing and my life.

Acknowledgements

Special thanks to my wife Vivian for her support for my writing career. To my extended family and in-laws, *meda mo ase*.

Kofi Akpabli, David Donkor, Kodwo Abban-Mensah, Henrietta Hammond-Boadu, Ben Dotsei Malor, Joseph Omotayo, Isaac Marion S-Darko, Isaac Neequaye and Vera Viva Nkrow, I am grateful for your editorial and proof-reading work. I am also indebted to Qouphy Appiah Obirikorang, Abubakar Ibrahim and Kwame Gyan for their input into this project in diverse ways.

I have had great support, ideas, feedback and correction from my friends on Facebook. Most of these stories here were literally cooked and refined on the online canvas of Facebook. The names are too many to mention, thank you all.

Nana A Damoah
September 2011
www.nanadamoah.com

Also by Nana Awere Damoah

THROUGH THE GATES OF THOUGHT

EXCURSIONS IN MY MIND

PRAISE FOR
TALES FROM DIFFERENT TAILS

There are many works by writers of mind-boggling intellectual ingenuity. Nana Awere Damoah is of a different breed of writers: he is not only a mind-boggler but also a literary nurse of the convalescent mind. He is an author of boundless creativity, whose wit like a brush, paints a beautiful picture of an analytic world that fuses fiction and reality. If there is a simple, objective term to describe him, he is simply an intellectual rebel who invests in a new world of endless creativity. Nana succeeds in taking his reader to a high level of abstraction about life without the usual uneasy sense of guilt that comes with rebelling against established norms.

Business and Financial Times

Nana Awere Damoah's stories have a way of taking us way back to the villages where we all have our beginnings, through University years laced with excitement and longing, and then dropping us right in the middle of bustling city life with its hustlers and everyday people struggling to earn a cedi. Each story is replete with lessons, for readers - sometimes tough, other times hopeful and after reading *Tales from Different Tails* one is left with the sense of having lived so many lives, of having encountered so many personalities. What a delightful collection!

Ayesha Harruna Attah, Author of Harmattan Rain

I have just thoroughly enjoyed reading *October Rush* and found it full of wit, suspense, empathy and humor. Well done to Nana, for so easily transporting me back to my university days with such vivid descriptions of characters, scenes and events. I can't wait to buy copies of the book as gifts to my non-Ghanaian friends to give them a brilliant glimpse into one aspect of Ghanaian college or university life.

Ben Dotsei Malor, Communications Advisor, United Nations, formerly of BBC World Service

Nana Awere Damoah's *Tales from Different Tails* encapsulates the everyday life of an African. His choice of words are 'magical' and the graphic mental picture is eccentric. This is a must-read for lovers of African literature.

Fidelis Mbah, News Correspondent, BBC World Service

I started the first story October Rush and couldn't put the book down. Made me wish I went to University in Ghana. The words used to describe events and people felt like I was watching a movie. What can I say - titillating!

Mariska Taylor-Darko: Author - The Secret to Detoxifying your Life and Love, Rhythms of Poetry in Motion and A Widow Must Not Speak

To read Nana Awere Damoah's classics, you need a quiet place and a good drink. Reading this classic, I was on a journey with Nana's characters, rediscovering the simple pleasures in life, wishing life could always be like what he writes, definitely a must read! Nana is a great writer always seeing the lighter side of life. NAD, thank you!

Whitney Boakye-Mensah: Events Planner, Entertainment Critic and Broadcast Journalist

Nana Awere Damoah's style of writing is impeccable, waxing his stories with no efforts; lacing each line with enough pun, humor and anecdotes that will even make the humor-deprived father-of-ten beam proudly with smile knowing that there's hope for the future. *Tales From Different Tails* is a must-have book for every literature addict, anyone looking for a new lease of life in African Literature and the general reading populace. The Surgeon-General recommends *Tales From Different Tails* for people with cardiac problems caused by both known and unknown factors as the book is scientifically proven to contain antioxidants and other mineral-rich elements.

Qouphy Appiah Obirikorang, Writer/ IT Professional

Tales from Different Tails is written in a free-flowing, conversational style which all will find easy to follow. Start reading and you are transported back into the "good old days" of schooling and small town life, when we were still discovering ourselves and carving niches for the future. Nana Damoah writes in a style reminiscent of the late Merari Alomele of Sikaman Palaver fame, and his writing is liberally dosed with Ghanamanisms, proverbs and metaphors unique to the Ghanaian society. Be prepared to call up your friends from college days to have a good laugh.

Jemimah Etornam Kassah, Trondheim, Norway

Nana Awere Damoah's *Tales from Different Tails* is an easy read; some stories made me laugh out and other left me thinking. The stories bring back memories of life on campus and give an interesting look into some things we go through in life as a whole; from feeling overwhelmed on your first day on campus through feeling like fresh meat left out with flies all over you in handling heart matters as a female on and off campus, to dealing with the everyday life of taking troski. Nana Awere Damoah uses words that make it easy for people from all age groups to read and understand, and injects humor which makes you want to keep reading. I really enjoyed this book.

Henrietta Hammond-Boadu, IT Professional

Having read Nana Awere's two previous books, *Through the Gates of Thought* and *Excursions in my Mind,* I was looking forward to another riveting read and truly I haven't been disappointed! Indeed, tales from different tails. From the interesting business of finding love on a typical university campus to the exhausting but, sometimes, hilarious task of using public transport in Ghana, Nana Awere uses his excellent story telling skills to talk about everyday life situations through his fascinating characters. Be prepared to be serenaded by Inte Gorang, the hopeful lovers Araba and Kwesi, and encounter the wily aplanke Akwasi. Well, what can I say? 'Thumps up!' Nana Awere Damoah.

Yvonne Amenuvor, Nurse, Avid Reader

If you thought the good old days of Ama Atta Aidoo are over, think again. *Tales from Different Tails* is totally different, refreshing, savvy and very Ghanaian. It is beautifully punctuated with some very real and identifiable African youth situations. Great story lines, sweeping clichés, easy to follow themes, funny punch lines and remarkable characters to remember long after you have read the stories. Ghanaian literature elevated. This is a must read for any lover of literature anywhere in the world!

Abubakar Ibrahim, Freelance Writer, Public Relations Practitioner

Everyday happenings written in simple language. Every sub-topic is as true as the word. The issue of grabbing reminds readers of how University students struggle to get attached to the opposite sex so as not to be left out of the fun or troubles associated with it. And as for the troski wahala, any Ghanaian who has not had a feel of it is missing out. It is the only platform where everybody on it has a say - the educated and uneducated alike. Keep it up.

Peggy Ama Donkor, Journalist of the Year (Ghana, 2005)

Like wine, Nana A Damoah is getting better with age. He has outgrown the mediocrity of virginity and is now writing with the aplomb of a veteran. His new book is like what a cigarette is to a smoker. If you don't want to get hooked to it, don't start it.

Panganai Chatapura, South Africa

With interesting stories like *Project Akoma, Dribble de Zagidibogidi* and

October Rush, Nana engages his readers' attention with very vivid descriptions and a great sense of humor. For most parts of my reading, I found myself imagining the scenes. For someone who didn't attend a traditional Ghanaian university, I was particularly thrilled with *October Rush*. Tales of Different Tails is a fantastic book that readers can really relate to. I have fallen in love with Nana Awere Damoah's art of storytelling!

Vivian Affoah, Journalist

A masterful survey of contemporary Ghanaian society with stories that touch and tickle in equal measure. Where Damoah excels is in drawing well rounded characters, setting them free on the page and observing the dynamic, intricate relationships that ensue.... a must read for this year.

Tendai Huchu, Author of 'The Hairdresser of Harare, Zimbabwe

Stunning! A fresh addition to the growing body of magnificent writing from Africa.

Geoff Gyasi, Book Blogger (Geosi Reads)

These stories are panoplies of boulders shaped and molded by the currents that drive Nana Awere Damoah's distant and close experiences. *Tales from Different Tails* is an ingenious craft linking past with present and core issues with words. The tales streamed over pages in this book are bolstered by the author's duteous attentiveness to details.

Joseph Omotayo, Writer, Book Blogger

In this collection of stories, Nana Damoah, once again, makes the ageless art of African story-telling attractive. *'Tales from Different Tails'* weaves a diversity of refreshingly familiar sceneries to portray the rich tapestry of African culture, employs humor to espouse timeless lessons, and adopts simple language to subtly reveal the complexities of the human nature. This book will teach you, encourage you, comfort you and set you thinking.

Theo Aryee, Banker, Poet

I found *October Rush* to be an entertaining rendering of University life in Ghana. Your characters' plights are easy to relate with, and for those who've passed through the Ghanaian university system, *October Rush* will, no doubt, bring back fond memories of various escapades similar to those of your characters. While the end of the story was largely expected, you included a little twist that brought all the characters full circle.

Empi Baryeh, Writer, Author of upcoming book 'Chancing Faith'

Every age has its geniuses who are blessed with the ability to bring meaning to African cultural life. Nana Awere Damoah does this through incredible story telling spiced with humour, passion and with the sharp eye of an ardent social observer. *Tales from Different Tails* is a clarion call not only to reminisce but also to reach for the insights of current contemporary Ghanaian cultural life. My favourite in this wonderful collection of stories is *"Face To Face – Tro Tro Palaver"*. In the time it takes to smile and nod at the musings of the characters, Nana Damoah has skilfully moved in for the coup de grace leaving me wanting more.

Nii Thompson, Editor, MyWeku.com

Tales from Different Tails is filled with the descriptive detail of an observant anthropologist, the literary reinvention of the legendary trickster, Kwaku Ananse, combined with the humor of everyday life in Ghana. Nana Awere Damoah is gradually settling into his role as a muse of his generation.

Dr Harry Odamtten, Assistant Professor, African and Atlantic History, Santa Clara University, U.S.A.

FOREWORD – TICKLING THE TALES

Each time a writer digs into his resources and brings out a story, humanity is largely, well- served. But it first begins with curiosity and plenty of generosity. In other words, one must first be interested in observing the human situation, and care enough to share. Tales from Different Tails sets out exactly to achieve this. In this selected work of fiction, Nana Awere Damoah gifts the world with his and our story and tells them in terms that enable us relate effectively. Set in contemporary Ghanaian society, the stories are themed on fate, romance, love and camaraderie betrayed.

There is an inherent relationship between mankind and the literary phenomenon known as the 'story'. This link is instinctive, almost biological. Whether told by the African fire-side setting or from the Western-styled Uncle Arthur's bedside, every child grows up loving tales of adventure and intrigue. In any narrative, the phrase 'once upon a time…' is one that tickles the ear and prepares us for the juice of news.

The truth, really, is that we live in a world that floats on stories. Functionally, story-telling is very much what nearly all the professions do. Explaining this is not a hard nut: the simplest form of sharing information is through story-telling.

Take journalists. After they have researched and gathered news materials they have got to tell the story. Same with our scientists, historians, statisticians, teachers and preachers. To a non-negotiable extent, the success of these vocations depends on how well they tell their stories.

Happily, in *Tales from Different Tails,* the stories are very well told. Indeed, what the author has done is to use the story telling techniques of the various professions to thrust the plots forward. The result is a compact, adrenaline-driven, easy-to-read work.

The main setting for many of the episodes is the university campus. The tertiary level is the last formal arena for preparing our leaders for various fields of encounter. The interactions and experiences that take place behind those walls are, thus, instructive for a nation.

The author shows an understanding of human insight such that he is able to switch the narrative voice from the girl on campus, to the street hustler and then the medical doctor; all in virtually one breath. His use of relevant concepts and jargons helps to unlock the door to a world all its own.

This book makes the ordinary worth celebrating. In part, the author fuels his narratives on nostalgia. For someone who happened to have grown up in the Accra Newtown-Kotobabi area myself, the landmarks and encounters are truly a home drive to familiar warmth.

All told, *Tales from Different Tails* is also serious commentary on societal shortfalls. It is the story of a nation that has not done very well for the citizenry. Facilities such as public transport and public places of convenience make mockery of our human dignity. This book also teaches that trust is a must, betrayal does not pay and love is beautiful.

But that is not all. There is a bonus that runs through. Humor. In this delightful work, Nana Awere Damoah demonstrates that he has a soft spot for the funny side and, (to the advantage of the reader) he has much difficulty keeping this to himself.

As people of a great heritage, we have to tell our stories- each of them, all of them. For this is a culture that leads to the road of self-knowledge…critical for the national development agenda.

KOFI AKPABLI

CNN African Journalist for Arts and Culture
(Winner for 2010 and 2011)

TALES

October Rush   27

Truth Floats   49

Dribble de Zagidibogidi   73

Hope Undeferred   85

Kojo Nkrabeah   101

Guardian of the Rented Well   117

Face to Face – Trotro Palaver   129

Project Akoma   143

OCTOBER RUSH

AKUA

ina was a timid girl, the sort whose timidity enhanced her looks. She appeared stressed and it was clear she needed a listening ear. As a leader in our hall fellowship, I was an appropriate downloading site for her worries, one to offer the occasional comfort and advice. My presence in the room at that moment was in response to a note she had left for me: could she talk to me, please, urgently? She had been there three times already, without luck since I kept a busy schedule and hardly studied in my room. She didn't keep me waiting, and appeared on schedule, taut and ready to explode. I tried to put her at ease, but everything I did seemed inconsequential; it was clear all she wanted was to get the issue off her chest. I braced myself for what she had to say. After hesitating a few minutes, during which I dug deeper into my chair and tried not to stare, encouraging her in silence, she blurted:

"It's the boys! They are pestering me, and I just can't cope!"

It was about three weeks into the new academic year and the campus was under the siege of the phenomenon known as the "October Rush". A new academic year brought many changes, and most significantly, it brought fresh female students who were termed in campus speak, as *New Stock*. The *continuing* (or senior) female students had various tags too. Second year ladies were *Reduced to Clear*, and the third/final year students belonged to the *Buy one, Get one free* category.

Campus wisdom held that the beginning of the first semester was generally the best time to *shop* for desirable ladies, freshers in this instance, before they got acclimatized. I looked knowingly at my guest; the *Rush* was on, evidently.

"Sister Akua, you see, I am confused already. Is it a sin to be fresh and beautiful in this university?" she lamented.

Fresh? Beautiful? *Eish!* Wasn't she a tad too confident of her looks? Or was it arrogance? But the words that came out of my mouth gave no hint of my thoughts. "Of course not. But take heart and tell me exactly what is driving you up the wall."

Nothing could have prepared the poor girl for such an experience. Many a first year student became perplexed in the maze of activities crowded into the first month of the academic year. Orientation programs, registration procedures, accommodation search, getting used to new lecture schedules, learning to find one's way about the large campus and preparing for matriculation – it was all unnerving for a fresher.

"Sister Akua, take this *Archito* guy (student of Architecture). He is in the second year and in Katanga. I met him on the STC bus when I was coming to Kumasi and we struck a good conversation. Now he's taken to visiting my room every other day. He is cool, handsome, and speaks good English. He's already been of immense help and has devoted a lot of his time showing me around campus. My room-mates say he is smooth and I shouldn't lose guard. He has already proposed and says he is coming to visit this weekend for his answer. I mean he was my first friend here on campus, but I'm not sure I'm ready for anything deeper at this point."

It was a Thursday evening and I had a scheduled a discussion with my room-mate Adwoa. She dropped in, saw how intense our conversation was, and merely changed her attire. I signalled that I would be following her to the Games Room as soon as I was done. The fresher looked at me with sad eyes before continuing.

"Then there is this guy I met at Paa Joe during the joint prayer meeting the Student Chaplaincy Council organized in the first week. He showed up to accompany me to the program every evening and has been visiting me regularly ever since. He hasn't said anything yet but, sister, actions speak louder than words. He is always sharing scripture with me and I learn he is a powerful Christian brother. Well, I respect him for his life and brotherly affection, but I can sense he wants more. He becomes visibly uncomfortable whenever he comes across me talking with other guys and sulks the rest of the day."

INTE GORANG

Inte Gorang stood in front of the mirror, putting finishing touches to his make-up. He turned this way and that way, brought his palm close to his mouth, fingers pointing upwards and exhaled through his mouth to sniff his breath. Yes, the mint breath freshener was working perfectly. His shirt was well-starched and ironed, the edges razor-sharp, the texture almost brittle. His hair shone from the *Sportin' Waves* cream he had judiciously applied. Yellow, the shoe shine boy, had ensured that one could see his image looking up from the flat top of Inte Gorang's shoes. A few sprays of his designer perfume used only for the most important occasions, and Joe Pabitey was ready for the evening's visit to Africa Hall.

Joe Pabitey. Few people called him by his real name. His nickname Inte Gorang was adulterated from John Garang, the Sudanese rebel leader. His friends teased that Joe Pabitey had been fighting for years, four years actually, to get an *inte,* a girlfriend on campus. Such persistence was both admired and jeered, and every time he approached the Porter's Lodge immaculately dressed, he was sure to receive applause and, sometimes, blessings, from his Katanga Hall colleagues. A few times, as he turned up the hill towards the Great Hall, the chorus of a song composed for him by his hall mates followed in his wake…

Ma ensi wo yie
Inte Gorang eeei
Inte rebel leader eei
Fa nkunim die bra nne!

to wit, "May it go well with you, Inte Gorang, Inte rebel leader, bring victory back today!"

Now in his final year, Gorang was bent on avoiding the proverbial *four-zero*, the term used to describe students who completed their four year degree courses without getting hitched, without *grabbing*. Along the way he had become a veteran of the October Rush. And each year, after failing to win a province, he had returned doggedly to the drawing board to re-strategize. His advances were not limited to the freshers though. It was just that having failed to succeed in the past three years, he had decided to really focus on freshers this final year. It was his last battle, going for the kill, do or die, be victorious or die trying!

In furtherance of this strategy, he had returned to campus two clear weeks before re-opening and befriended all the porters in the female and mixed halls. With heavy tipping, almost amounting to bribing, he had secured their tacit agreement to note down all the nice girls and their room numbers, so he wouldn't have to waste time doing reconnaissance. By the time school re-opened and the freshers started arriving for the orientation program, he had been on the Accra route more than four times, journeying back to Kumasi on the STC buses, to get acquainted with some of the ladies at the bus terminals. With such rich experience, he could pick out the freshers with ease – their large suitcases, parents dropping them off and anxious at their departure, eager conversations on mobile phones, and more private information obtained from discreet eavesdropping.

He was extra helpful to them and once they got to Tech junction, he ensured that he was visibly available to get them taxis to campus, a coincidental good Samaritan to the freshers – all part of the warlord's battle plan.

BAZOOK

It was convenient for him to be a resident of the Independence Hall. The hall's proximity to the University's stadium (popularly known as Paa Joe) suited him well for he loved to pray in the open expanse. Brother Bazook was very prayerful, an ardent Christian who spent at least two hours each day interceding for souls and his nation, his foremost prayer topics. He earned his nickname when he acted in a play at church. In that drama, he role-played what he loved doing in real life: praying. In one of the scenes, he led a group of *ogyacious* or zealous Christians in prayer and called on them to "shoot the devil" with spiritual intercontinental ballistic and other long-range missiles. That was in the years just after the first Gulf War. As the leader of that counter-terrorist army, he naturally employed the bazooka and thus his nickname Bazook.

He was in the third year and a relationship with one of the ladies was the last thing on his mind. Brother Bazook was too spiritual for that kind of carnal indulgence. Brother Bazook was known to have exorcised the demon of carnality from another brother when the latter

31

simply asked him for bread, rebuking him; "When souls are perishing, you are thinking of bread!"

During the first week of his third year, Bazook had just spent two hours at Paa Joe, praying in tongues and interceding for souls. He felt really fulfilled, satisfied he had done his Christian duty, as he rounded up his prayers around 8.30 pm. As he climbed up the stairs to cross the street and take the footpath through the Annex Block, he espied a guy sitting by the security check post. He walked on, until he heard the guy walking behind him, calling his attention before striding up to catch up with him.

"Brother, God bless you for your prayers. May I ask what you were praying about?"

Bazook smiled at the stranger, wondering: "Perhaps he wants to tap into my passion for souls?"

"Well, I was interceding for souls this evening."

The stranger responded, "Brother, the Spirit intercedes for us with groans we cannot understand, and He knows our real heart's desires. I can interpret tongues and all I heard you say for two hours I have been here at Paa Joe was 'Lord, give me a wife!' That is the true desire of your heart, even though you may try not to listen to that inner voice." Just as he appeared, the stranger said a quick goodnight and disappeared into the night in the opposite direction.

Bazook spent that night reflecting deeply. Indeed, he had begun to think about relationships lately, much as he tried to push the subject out of his mind. Perhaps, God had used the stranger to tell him it was OK to have such thoughts, they may not be carnal after all? Perhaps he wasn't supposed to be a Paul? A spiritual Peter was also in the Bible.

As he reflected, it hit him hard that it was October. The Rush. Yes, there is, The Rush!

PATTY

The length of the queue behind your door is a reflection of your popularity as a fresh girl during October Rush, she had been told. She knew she was beautiful. That fact had been forcefully appreciated whilst she was in Wesley Girls, in Cape Coast. During the InterCo (inter colleges) competitions, she had the most enquiries from the boys from Kwabotwe, Adisco and Augusco, much to the chagrin of her friends, who tried very hard to hide their envy. It got to a point where she had to play pranks on those boys to keep them off. She always recalled one particular incident with mirth.

The guy, from Kwabotwe, had pestered her the entire duration of one competition, for two days. From all indications, he was not used to being *bounced*, one of those boys who felt every girl should melt at the mention of his name like Blue Band margarine under the onslaught of a hot knife. He just wouldn't take "No" for an answer. And by then, she, Patty Sutherland-Graves, had learnt that for such boys only humiliation would teach them that even though all heads may look the same, the thoughts in them differ.

On the second day, she grudgingly acquiesced and gave him her name; he wanted to visit her at school. She told him she was called Pat Ricia and they agreed for him to visit – two weeks later, on the girls' visiting day.

33

On the appointed day, Alan Quartey – for that was the guy's name, she could never forget it – duly turned up and asked for *Miss Pat Ricia*. By prior arrangement, the request filtered to Patty's friends who took Alan to the Assembly Hall and gave him a seat at the center of the main stage, with the promise of informing *Miss Ricia* of his arrival. Back in the dormitory, Patty and her friends were rolling across the floor in laughter, completely overcome by the hilarity of it! The guy was clearly a *toke-* a dimwit, to come asking after a Pat Ricia! Her friends took turns passing by the Hall, ostensibly to search for a missing item or to look for a friend, the main purpose being to have a look at the latest *toke* to visit their campus.

After about two hours of waiting in vain for Miss Ricia to appear, Alan Quartey got the message and left, with his tail in between his legs.

Patty was a veteran at playing love games and had arrived on campus for her first year well aware of the October Rush and eager to partake. Clearly, she would not be on the receiving end.

Akua

We were sitting on the lower bunk of the bed. I got up and went to the fridge to pick two bottles of Fanta, opened both and gave one to Tina. I insisted when she refused the drink. I had been out studying the whole day and needed to boost my sugar level; perhaps I needed the drink more than she but it wouldn't do any harm for her to relax a bit more.

"What you are experiencing is called the October Rush, it is seasonal and it will pass. Tina, the question to ask is: Are you ready for any relationship at this time in your life?"

"No, not really."

"But you do appreciate that you cannot fend off young men forever, and that you will have to make a decision one day, don't you?"

"Oh yes, I do. It is just that now with all of them coming towards me at the same time, I feel confused, like a pollen-laden flower in the land of a thousand bees!"

"Yeah, that's right and we all experienced it. The important thing is to ascertain whether any of these guys – and there will be more, I can assure you – is serious and will still be around after the Rush. Some of the guys see it as a game, some are also serious. Some of the guys come your way accidentally, others encounter you by plan. We will have to see how it goes. On the other hand, there are some girls who also take advantage of guys during the Rush and even after.

"One of such girls was my room-mate in first year, Christabel. If ever there was a female player, she was one. Christy could wind the hearts of men like a Bonwire kente master weaver! Her tongue was sweeter than the honeycombs of Babylon and her tales more intricate than those of legendary Kweku Ananse. All the guys who came proposing to her were accepted, none of them suspected they had rivals, and each of them thought he was the only one on the throne of her heart. Her admirers were not only students; lecturers, businessmen and teaching assistants had their names in her catalogue. She often said you needed some for study support, some to pay your bills, some to fund your shopping, and some just to take you out to functions. So she grouped her love-struck or highly-infatutaed admirers to facilitate various relevant categories of need. There was one who took care of her educational needs only. Another existed in her life just to provide finance. Other took care of "tourism" needs and public affairs. She even had a guy whose main use was ironing! I always pitied that guy.

"Christabel would chat with him deep into the night, usually on Sunday, and then around midnight, she would make an attempt to touch her mound of dresses to be ironed for the week. This guy would immediately get up and insist on ironing! Christabel would smile sweetly, call him a darling and, a few minutes later, go to sleep, whilst the poor guy continued the ironing. He would finish at dawn, let himself out of the room and be back for the same routine the next week. Oh what love could push some men to do!

"One day, when he was almost done with the ironing, it started raining heavily. It was around 2 a.m. Christabel looked outside and decided that seeing how heavy the rain was, the guy should sleep in our room, and go to his hall early in the morning. The guy stepped out – we thought he was going to the gents, ok, ladies in this case. Twenty minutes later, there he was all wet, clutching a large cloth in his hands. He had rushed to his hall to pick up his sleeping cloth! It just confirmed my belief that he had a few wires incorrectly connected upstairs!"

"Room five-eight! Room five-eight!"

That was my room-mate, Adwoa, calling from the P-Lodge. I stepped out of the room and looked down from the rails. There was a guy standing with her, who I recognized immediately as Brother Bazook.

"Roomie, Bra Bazook here is looking for Tina, and I told him she was with you."

Tina? Was Bazook one of the contenders for the young girl's heart?

"Ei, Bra Bazook, so if it wasn't for Tina, you wouldn't have even asked of me, eh?"

"Sister Akua, it is not like that oh, just that mankind has been spending more time on souls, interceding and following up. I have an urgent message to deliver to the daughter of God, Tina."
"OK, she will be down with you soon, or you want to come up here to see her?"

Tina had by now joined me on the corridor and indicated that he should wait for her at the P-Lodge, and we both returned to my room.

"Do you know Brother Bazook?" I asked Tina. She nodded.
"He is the *Chrife* or Christian Fellowship brother I told you about. I like him as a brother-in-Christ, but nothing more. If he should propose today, I will reject him, but how does one bounce such a brother without hurting his feelings? I can tell his affection is genuine and he is passionate, and I am certain he doesn't go around proposing to lots of ladies…I could even be the first."

At this point, I had to decide whether to follow my head or my heart. I will tell you why. I knew Brother Bazook well and always secretly admired him. Indeed, my room-mate was the first person who noted how my face lit up anytime he visited us in our room, and how many times I mentioned him in our conversations. Adwoa once challenged that she believed I was falling in love with Brother Bazook. I rebuked her, saying that I was just appreciating his spirituality and love for the Lord's work. Upon reflection, however, I had at least admitted in my heart – yes, I felt more than sisterly affection towards Bazook. He had been a friend for three years, but these mushy feelings had begun to be acknowledged just about a year ago. The problem was that Bazook seemed to "see girls as trees", as Adwoa usually said. On the other hand, how does a Christian girl go about letting a brother know that she loved him and was just waiting for him to pop the question, without appearing like a bone going after the dog?

Tina's fond words about Bazook therefore hit me, making me momentarily lose my concentration.

"Yes…yes, er what did you say? Oh yes, I know Bazook as someone who rarely expresses interest in girls. If he is developing some affection towards you, he must be serious then. Perhaps he even has a prophecy to that effect. Go on, go and talk to him."

INTE GORANG

Gorang typically got to Africa Hall just after 9pm. Being an all-female hall of residence meant Africa Hall attracted a good amount of visits from men with a mission. As experienced as he was, he knew that most of the guys rarely visited girls after 9pm. The period between 9pm and midnight was usually reserved for those closest to the girls – boyfriends, relatives, girlfriends. Where boyfriends were concerned, it was called *owner's time*. So for the brave, that period was free and if you were lucky to be admitted and no one was with your object of interest, you had monopoly time to make your point and pitch.

Gorang was visiting two girls this time: Patty and Tina. The former was a tough nut, while the latter was generally easy, he reckoned. The tactic was to spend more time on the tougher subject and then finish off with the easier target.

Gorang climbed the stairs up to the fifth floor and stopped to lean on the railing, to catch his breath. The lifts had never worked in the four years he had been on campus. Both the hunter and the hunted suffer almost equally, he thought, as he continued his walk up to the eighth floor. When he turned left towards Room 808, and saw six guys leaning on the railings on the eighth floor, he briefly wondered whether they were going up to the rooftop, what for he couldn't fathom. Perhaps a prayer meeting? As he passed behind them and drew closer to the door of Room 808 to knock, he felt a gentle tap on his shoulder.

"Are you going there to see anyone?"

He turned to see the face of one of the guys he had passed, waiting on the corridor.

"Yes, I am here to see Patty, she is in Room 808."
"Then please join the queue, we are all here to see her."

"Come in please."

Patty was waiting. That was two hours later, but Gorang knew it was part of the game. With patience, one could kill an ant, dissect it and take out its heart, he soliloquized, as he opened the door and entered the room, taking his turn in the bidding arena.

BAZOOK

"When the Bible talks about offering yourself as a living sacrifice, holy and acceptable, it includes even your choices. Make sure that what you choose does not become a scar on you and a hindrance to your Christian living," Bazook exhorted Tina.

Tina was both shy and afraid of Brother Bazook at the beginning of their friendship, but with the passage of time, she was learning to relax in his presence. He, in turn, was increasingly loosening up enough to speak contemporary biblical English, instead of the King James version he utilized during the first week she met him. Tina remembered with mirth how he used to intersperse his speech with "Thou knowest", instead of "You know". They were standing under the trees that bordered the street leading to Africa Hall and, as usual, Bazook was sharing some nuggets, as he called them, from his Bible reading that day.

Tina's earlier discussion with Sister Akua had been helpful, and whilst descending the stairs to the P-Lodge to meet Bazook, she had decided to take matters in her own hands and stop acting docile. She had a right to decide who stressed her out, and who she wanted to get close to her. She recalled Sister Akua's words that the decision was hers to make one day. She decided that day would not be in her first semester.

"Brother Bazook, can I ask you a question?"
"Of course, Tina."
"You see, a number of boys have been showing affection for me in a nice way, during these past few weeks on campus…"
"Ei, I hope I am not counted in that list o!" Bazook burst out laughing.
Shyly, "Well, to be truthful, you are!"

Bazook continued laughing.

"Ok, Ok," Tina struggled to get him to concentrate, "now back to my question. How can one ascertain that the love a man professes is genuine? If you love a girl, how do you show it, Bazook? Have you ever loved a girl? Can you fall in love within a couple of weeks and be clear that you want to have a life-long commitment?"
"*Ebei*, Tina, why? You want to set a GCE A-Level question or what?"

This triggered another round of laughter, with Bazook clutching his stomach.

41

"Well, let's take it one at a time then, Tina. Yes, I have loved a girl, and still love her. And, no, even though I have shown you great affection during these few weeks, my motives are purely sisterly, nothing else."
"I see."

"Indeed, first advice and this was given to girls by our Scripture Union patron: never assume a boy's love. Let it be expressed first."
"But what if it is quite clear from the boy's actions that he is just waiting for the right time to propose, Bazook? What if it is obvious from the amount of time he spends on you, the number of notes he sends you, the little gifts he sometimes sends across?"

"Still, don't assume, Tina. My view is that a guy who really loves you will not be afraid to lose you during the October Rush, and may not rush you during the period either. That person will possibly become your friend, not too obtrusive or interfering, so as not to risk alienation. So, true, the person may 'fall in love' with you, but the maturing time for that love definitely will outlive the October Rush."
"OK, good points there. You still haven't answered one question, though."

"*Eish*, Tina, today you really want to grill me, huh? Don't you know that if I am heard discussing these things with you, I could be tagged 'carnal'? You know, you are one of the few girls who is able to get me to discuss these deep topics *o o*."
"Wow that is nice. But perhaps from you I can get unalloyed truth about these questions. So now back to the question: how do you show your love to a girl?"
"Tina!" She could almost swear he was blushing.
"Bazook! Ha-ha, answer the question, brother."

PATTY

"Do you have a car?"

"Er, no."

"Are you staying in one of the hostels on campus, like Brunei or Gaza and how many are you in your room?"

"I am in Katanga. You know, in the old days, final year students had a room each to themselves, but these days, two of us have to share. Hmm, tough days now *koraa*…"

"How many are you in your room?"

"OK, we are two officially…"

"Total number in your room?"

"…and we have two perchers."

"Do you have a fridge and a microwave in your room? What is the size of the TV in your room – is it a plasma or a 21-inch set?"

"When was the last time you travelled abroad?"

"Which restaurants do you visit frequently in Kumasi, I don't mean on campus?"

Forty-five minutes later, Gorang had to come up with an excuse. He left Room 808 dejected. *Eish*, what frightening heights the Rush game had reached! He was clearly not in Patty's league, and he didn't even know if he had enough energy to see Tina. Besides, it was late.

As he exited the P-Lodge, providence and fate combined to present Tina to him. She was just about to ascend the stairs to her block.

"Hello, helloooo, Tina!" Gorang called.

"Hi Joe." The name Inte Gorang hadn't filtered to her yet.

"I was coming to see you but something came up in the hall, so couldn't set off early. That is why I am late."

"Ah, but you just descended from Block B. If you really were coming to see me urgently, wouldn't you have been descending from Block A, where my room is?"

Eish, the first year girls this year are wild *o o,* Gorang thought. A bad night it was turning out for him. A smooth operator, he didn't miss a beat.

"That is what I was coming to. Actually, the *something* I spoke about had to do with a project work. So I had to work on it, and submit to my project mate in 504, and she detained me to do some explanation too."

"Alright, I understand now. So what did you want to discuss with me, Joe? Please make it snappy, as I have had a long day and feeling tired."

"Well, Tina, you must have realized that with such beauty as has been bestowed on you, any man with a working brain cannot pass you without a second or even a third glimpse. I have been glancing plenty times! These past few weeks, each day that passes reinforces the love I have developed for you, even beyond the outer beauty. Your character, your smile; your intelligent conversations, your style; all these have combined to sweep me off my feet. It has been difficult holding back this expression…"

"Joe, thanks, but this is about the fifth such poetry I have heard this week. Besides my beauty, can you give me five proper reasons why I should believe you, and can you wait for another month to see if these reasons still hold?"

Gorang had a fitful sleep that night. It had been a bad day.

IN THE END...

It actually turned out that Brother Bazook was interested in Akua, and the discussion with Tina teased him out of his shyness. Tina turned out to be his consultant. When Akua accepted his proposal, Tina later told Akua Bazook came straight afterwards to her room, speaking in his own tongues!

Gorang completed his degree, four-zero.

Patty *bounced* most of the bidders, settling for a married Kumasi business tycoon. When the tycoon's wife returned to Ghana two years later, he dropped Patty, who was in her third year. She got onto the ranks of BOGOF – Buy one, Get one Free.

Tina got hitched to a classmate of hers, in her third year. He had his own stories of chasing women, and getting wounded by some. In the university, he had become wiser and knew that most of the good girls didn't like being rushed. His name was Alan Quartey.

TRUTH FLOATS

lowing over the quiet ambience of the University campus, the cold harmattan winds did nothing to counter the heat in the packed Room 61M of Nyaniba Hall. Akoto envied his room-mate who slept on, snoring like a scooter whose exhaust pipe had burst, as if their room was a suite in the Ambassador Hotel. Kweku M. Ananse was his name and he was the most carefree person Akoto had ever seen. So full of life and ideas.

Kweku Ananse. The only son of his father. The senior Ananse, whose first name Owawani became synonymous with cunning in his village of Hiawa.

After five daughters, Owawani's desire for a male heir became so intense he almost cursed the gods. So when Kweku was born, his father Owawani was simply over the moon.

Before Kweku's birth, the elders of the Ablade clan, Owawani's family, had come to his house at dawn. The delegation of four elders was led by *Abusuapanyin* (clan-head) Kwaw Abora, a cranky old man of indeterminate age, who was famous for his sharp tongue and for getting straight to the point.

After the customary serving of water to welcome the guests, followed by some small talk – about the weather, the harvest, the chieftaincy disputes in the neighbouring villages – Owawani cleared his throat, a signal that he wanted to speak.

One of the elders, Mensu Kyekyeku, acted as the linguist of the visiting delegation and it was to him that Owawani addressed his opening words.

"Kyekyeku, let *Opanyin* Abora know that here in my house all is well. The elders say 'we may know yet we still ask, and that the matter from outside the house is usually sweeter than what is in the house'. You have come, kindly let me know your mission."

Kyekyeku turned to *Opanyin* Abora and relayed the message to him.

"Opanyin, this is what your son Owawani is asking; he says we have come, so he is eager to know what brought us here at this early hour when he should be doing what real men do before their wives wake up to sweep." The men roared with laughter.

Opanyin Abora called the meeting to order.

> "*Agoooo.*"
> "*Ameeee,*" the others responded.
> "*Agooo.*"
> "*Ameee.*"
> "*Anuanom, agooo.*"
> "*Ameee.*"

Opanyin Abora went straight to the meat of their mission: the family had taken note that Owawani's wife Eno Serwaa had been producing only girls. Investigations into her family had revealed that it wasn't unusual: most of her sisters had female offspring.

"Did the elders not say that when a woman makes a shield, it is stored in a man's room, and also that a woman may buy a shotgun but keeps it in the corner of a man's room? Owawani, we want you to take a second wife, so you can get a male heir. I am done." After a moment of clumsy silence and some extra small chatter, the visiting delegation departed just as suddenly as it arrived.

That was two years before Kweku Ananse was born, and Owawani was glad that he was proved right by sticking to his only wife Adjoa Serwaa, a moral victory for the man who otherwise considered morals the bread of cowards.

The hall clock, which was reputed to be as old as the University, chimed five times. The myth was that when the clock stopped chiming, the University would produce the premier first class student in Physics. And the story went that to prevent this, the Physics department set a tithe of its budget each year aside to ensure the clock was always in good shape. Akoto didn't mind that story much; all he cared for was that the clock was as reliable to offer the correct time as his room-mate and friend, Kweku, was being mischievous.

"*Massa*, wake up, wake up", Akoto tried to rouse Kweku from his sleep.

The man slept like a puff adder that slept both day and night because it couldn't distinguish between the two.

"Kweku! It is time to get ready for lectures!" Akoto persisted.
"Hmm, hmmm, won't man get any peace in this world at all? What is it, eh, what *koraa* is the matter?"
"Time for bathing, lazy booonnnnnneeessss!"
"*Kai*! And I haven't ironed too!"

With that, the Spiderman jumped from his bed. He was nicknamed the Spiderman because of his surname. At first, he wasn't too pleased with the alias, but after watching the movie *Spiderman*, he realized the character really epitomized what he, Kweku Ananse, could achieve: almost anything. To Kweku, the whole world was like a draught board and the smartest player could always win the game. The rules of the game were: the end justifies the means. It is only the squirrel who sang that things must be done in the right way. In the gospel according to Kweku Ananse, life was hard and the smart took it by force. His father had made it through life by being smart and the offspring of the long snake could not be short. The elders had advised that one should not be happy when people remark that you were a chip of the old block, because your father might have been a questionable character. But Kweku loved it so. He was indeed the Spiderman.

At birth, Kweku's father had looked intently at his son, searching for any resemblance; he found one immediately – the head, and particularly the back of the head. Many had described the back of Owawani Ananse's head as resembling that of a yawning bird. Owawani's retort had always been that it housed a brain of immense capabilities, and that was the same level of intelligence Owawani prayed for his son.

Owawani had chosen his son's name, as soon as he was told his wife had gone into labour at the hospital. He would call him Kweku Ananse. Kweku because he was born on a Wednesday. Ananse was the family name, the Akan word for spider.

The eighth day after the birth of the little boy, the *outdooring* took place to name him, to give him an identity. It is believed that before the eighth day, a newly born child was still in a dilemma whether to stay on earth or go back to the land of the ancestors. After eight days, one was quite sure then the child would stay, and it is at that point that the child was given a name. Before then, it was called *Hey*, an ambiguous name.

Egya Ananse, as the father was known by all, was a happy man on that day. In Hiawa, the name of the parent almost vanished as soon as kids were added to the family. The mother of Mansa became Mansa Maame, (or Mansa's Mother) and the father Mansa Papa. Now Owawani Ananse was called Kweku Papa, a name he relished as if he had earned it on the battlefield. His chest heaved at the mere thought of that. He could now take his rightful place under the nim tree where the men gathered to play draughts and discuss events after work, fortified with palm wine drank from calabashes. He had shown that his waist was not just for dancing and production of girls – he now had a boy to prove that his loins had come of age.

It was Tuesday, and they both met Ama Adoma at the Mecca bridge to escort her to lectures, hence the early rise.

Ama Adoma. The only one advantage his friend Akoto had over him. The prettiest girl he had ever seen in his fast life. Her neck was like a ringed sausage, earning her the name Ama Konfε, the girl with the beautiful neck. When she smiled, her checks reformed into two dimples, which could hold two pebbles at ease. Her lips parted to reveal teeth set neatly by each other like footballers arranged in a defence wall before a free kick, sparkling white like fresh cotton buds against background savannah grass. Her walk was like that of a graceful Adowa dancer. The most beautiful lady on campus and she was Akoto's fiancée.

A rich white sky laced with blue looked down on the earth that morning. It had rained the previous night and the streets were strewn with leaves and broken branches. The fragrance of earth, leaves, flowers, and soil permeated the ambience.

The grass still held morning dew, forming cute little droplets on the surfaces of the leaves. There was no wind, no sunshine. It was all serene, peaceful.

53

Adoma's face matched the spirit of the morning. As usual, it was radiant with joy. She sang as she descended the stairs of Yaa Asantewaa Hall, a song she had been singing from the bathroom.

> *When peace like a river*
> *Attended my way*
> *When sorrows like sweet billows roll*

She went through the great doors opposite the P-Lodge and into the street. Her heart was full of song and she was at peace. It felt good to be alive!

> *Whatever my lot*
> *Thou has taught me to say*
> *It is well, it is well*
> *With my soul*

Others on their way to lectures passed her by. Some waved and hurried on. She preferred to pass through Nkrumah Hall. The path under the trees was part of her route. As she went down the hilly plain towards the roundabout, Adwoa bypassed her. Her room-mate was always in a hurry. Adoma looked at her wrist watch, and realised she had enough time to move on at her normal pace.

> *It is well, it is well*
> *With my soul, with my soul*
> *It is well, it is well*
> *With my soul*

Kweku and Akoto were both in their final year at the University College of Amenfi, and had a final semester to go. Kweku was as evasive about his hometown as he was about the secondary school he attended; he didn't divulge much. When pushed to the wall to share a bit about himself, Kweku was known to say to his questioners that if you searched too deeply under the eyes of a corpse, you were certain to see a ghost. But his cunning and cleverness you couldn't take away from him. Sometimes, Akoto wondered whether his friend really sat for any examinations at all, before entering the University.

"Kweku, please hurry up. We are running late."

"Ho ho, you and your pushing with respect to Adoma, why? Is she a time-bomb? Will she explode if we don't get to her on time?"

"*Charlie*, you can play with your fiancée when you get one. As for me, I won't let any other person take away my girl with TLC – tender loving care. I will guard her like a multi-million dollar winning lottery ticket!"

"Even the Queen of England is not treated like your Adoma. Anyway, I am ready. Let me not be the reason for any break-ups. But remember, there is bound to be a knot in any long string."

On their way to the Mecca Bridge Hall, Akoto thought of what Kweku had said. Akoto's mum lived in the United Kingdom and so he travelled abroad on most vacations. His visa had already been obtained and he was due to travel right after his final examinations. He wanted to spend a couple of years abroad, slave away and come back to Ghana with enough resources to wed his queen. Even the vulture which is not edible nursed its eggs in the branches of a high tree, because man is hard to trust and eggs are delicacies!

Adoma was near the Mecca bridge now. A smile broke over her pretty face when she saw Akoto, with his faithful friend Kweku by his side. She linked her arms with his, and they continued to the lecture area.

Akoto didn't want to keep Adoma waiting too long after school before marriage and didn't want to be too far away from her. A glance at Adoma by his side reinforced his resolve to marry her in the shortest possible time.

"What a beauty", thought Kweku, as he also stole a glance at Adoma. His plans were still under construction within his mind. Wasn't it said that young people kept their money in the pocket of their parents?

Kweku had no problem with getting girlfriends, the problem was in retaining them. Kweku once went out with a girl called Akua Kyeiwaa. Kyeiwaa used to tell everyone - who cared to listen - that in her relationship with Kweku, she had to do all the work in maintaining and sustaining their relationship, likening it to the tail wagging the dog.

But Adoma was just so special, and he was beginning to like his best friend's fiancée a lot. A tooth lost its respect and place in an aching jaw and a nugget could never sparkle besides charcoal. Adoma was fit for him, Kweku, and have her he would. Only in the community of pregnant women does an over-matured coconut dropped on its own accord. Kweku was neither a pregnant woman nor was he living in such a community. He was the smartest man on campus and he would certainly pluck this ripe coconut – Adoma.

He knew he would have to call on all his skills and fertile schemes, and he was prepared for it. He didn't mind the fact that this could bring a rift between him and Akoto, because however kind a man was, he would not give his wife as a gift to his friend. So, he would bid his time and strike at the right time, for it was with patience that the experienced hunter killed an elephant. Kweku started feeling that he was entitled to Adoma, on the same level as Akoto. Wasn't he the go-between for the two lovebirds in the early days of their relationship and even now?

Didn't he help Akoto win Adoma? Indeed, a bedfellow in sowing the seed should be a part in the harvest, he reasoned. He didn't mind what people would say when he succeeded. Ethics, friendship, betrayal of trust, disloyalty - all stupid impediments! It was only the coward who was scared by the scarecrow, and Kweku believed that he wasn't a coward at all – no scheme was out of his bounds.

One day Adoma visited their room. Akoto wasn't in the room; he had a project proposal to defend. Adoma sat on Akoto's bed as she sipped the Coca Cola Kweku bought for her from the hall canteen.

"So, how are studies, Adoma?" Kweku asked.

"*Hmm*, not too bad oo. I am managing, but sometimes I get too stressed out with Economics. It is getting better though."

"OK, good. Tell me, Adoma, how are you going to sustain the love you have for Akoto when he travels? I understand long-distance relationships are difficult to maintain."

"Ah Kweku! When you love someone, distance doesn't matter oo, only love does."

"*Yoo*, my mouth is a bucket! Me, I am only asking. When a child sees the eyes of a crab, he mistakenly takes them for sticks."

Very soon, July came and it was time for Akoto to travel. On the departure day, Kweku, Adoma and Akoto travelled together to Accra for his flight. The parting was emotional; it was difficult for both Akoto and Adoma, and Kweku joined in their tears. In fact, he became the sympathiser who wept more than the bereaved. The owner of the house was going away, and a certain special responsibility was being thrust upon Kweku! Kweku was already devising his own plans; after all, he was no bodyguard who only protected a property without exploiting it.

When the final boarding call was made, Adoma rushed into Akoto's arms yet again. A flood of tears came gushing down from the banks of Adoma's eyes, and Akoto had to struggle this time not to join her. He smiled wryly when he remembered the saying that a man was not supposed to cry. Such difficult advice to follow when your loved one was weeping on your shoulders with emotions strong enough to even stir the chords of an executioner's heart!

Since Adoma was not staying in the city, and couldn't get letters through regular mail, Akoto decided that he would be writing frequently through Kweku.

"Akoto, my friend", Kweku promised, "I will do my best to ensure that communication between the two of you is not broken. After all, the mushroom and the hill have no thanks between them. They are one and the same. What is yours is mine to maintain for your sake."
"*Me d'ase*, Kweku. You have been such a good friend, and my heart is light knowing you are here for me."

This was the period just before mobile phones could be found in almost every village in the land.

Six months had passed since Akoto left, and Adoma was doing her National Service in Wasa Asikuma. She had received two or so letters in the initial months following his departure and then, nothing. For four months, she had not heard from Akoto at all. Kweku Ananse called her at the Post office weekly and always said Akoto was yet to send any new letter down for her.

After school each day, she took a walk along the road towards Ankonsia, alone with her thoughts. She walked alone usually, in silence, deep in thought, oblivious that it was getting dark, as the villagers returned from their farms, and waved at her. She hardly noticed them. She only thought of Akoto. Indeed, the elders were right when they said the mouth that was used to source a loan was not the same one used to pay it. Akoto had promised her heaven, and sworn to keep her in perpetual touch. Adoma was getting disappointed and was becoming increasingly disillusioned with Akoto. Her only consolation and source of strength in the hard times had been Kweku Ananse. Kweku Ananse, an object she was surprised to find herself having thoughts about.

Kweku's plan was working to perfection. Parcels were made to facilitate easy recovery. He made sure that with each visit and call to Adoma, his hidden message was easily deciphered. Initially, he had forwarded Akoto's letter to Adoma, to give her the impression that if Akoto should write, Ananse would promptly deliver the letters. He had even travelled the whole night to Asikuma, arriving at dawn, just to prove the point that he (Kweku) treated Akoto's letters with urgency.

But when two bosom friends vie for one and the same lady, they have chosen a common road to be each other's enemy. Kweku was determined to win this war. Kweku was the linguist in this affair, the middle man in this relationship. Did the elders not say that only the linguist could blow the chief's ivory horn to sing his Highness' eulogy? Kweku had decided to blow the horn and produce a tune favourable to him. So his plan was simple: to hold on to subsequent letters from Akoto to Adoma and also detain those from Adoma to Akoto. His weekly calls and occasional visits to Wasa increased.

"Kweku, this your friend, what sort of life is this? *Eh*, how can he treat me this way?" Adoma asked Kweku one afternoon in Asikuma.

It was in August, about a year following Akoto's departure and many months since Adoma heard from him.

"Adoma, the head is not a coconut that you can open to see what is inside it. Though he is my friend, I cannot explain all his actions," Kweku said, looking at the beautiful girl before him. Ah, such a beauty, Kweku said to himself the umpteenth time. How true it was that only a toothless cat would not lick his lips when a mouse was playing near his nose. Kweku was enjoying the game he was playing with this beautiful mouse and his lips were getting even worn out from all the licking!
"But Kweku, why? I have always been a faithful partner to your friend. And I have not given him any cause for him to treat me like this!"
"You can't understand some men. You usually don't know the worth of someone until she leaves you. In school, we had a prayer we prayed in the dining hall: some want, they don't get; some get they don't want..."
"But we want and we get so we thank thee oh Lord!" Adoma finished it.

They laughed together.

Adoma's tone turned serious: "Kweku, what do you mean by that?"
"Oh, no, nothing serious. Except that, to the blind, the antics of the monkey and his gesticulations would never be enough to excite. But the monkey would seriously entertain the discerning with the same dance!"

Kweku left that evening for Accra (that day he left earlier than usual because he said his bank was organizing a week long course for all its banking staff – Kweku was the Human Resource Officer or HRO, as many junior staff members simply called him). After his departure, Adoma chewed long and hard on his words. Was Kweku telling her that she was blind and not seeing how good he, Kweku, had been to her in those trying times? Kweku was good-looking and had been good, too good, to her. A bird in hand was worth two in the bush, and there was no use waiting for those two in the bush, especially when they still had wings to fly! Who knew what Akoto was doing in the United Kingdom?

"But Adoma, your love for Akoto has not evaporated, has it?" her inner voice debated with her.
"I know, I still love him. He is my first love, and it is very difficult to get over him. In fact, I am confused."

Her mind didn't give up its advocacy for Kweku.

"See, there is no one who has been faithful to you in these trying times than Kweku. Just consider how he comes regularly all the way to this village to see you. How many letters have you not written to Akoto? Tell me, how many of them has he replied? Tell me! When you asked Kweku to ask Akoto about the way forward, wasn't Akoto evasive?"
"Well, yes, that is what Kweku told me. I really don't know what to do!"

The spider worked tirelessly, spinning her web in the corner of the cubicle. It was a huge web with intricate designs. The spider worked silently, tired but hopeful - hopeful that good work will yield great dividends. Didn't the elders say that the one who should enjoy the meal is the one who laboured?

The fly was enjoying his flight through the nice ambience in the room. The day's peregrinations had been fruitful. He had travelled far and wide, and enjoyed various substrates. He was in high spirits and had already started looking forward to a good night's sleep. The wind was his friend, the air was his companion, and he knew no enemies. It has been said many times by the sages that our most vulnerable times are the immediate moments after victories or great successes. It can be added that after a good meal, one can also be vulnerable, and that was the state the fly was in.
It was with such warm thoughts and abandon that the fly flew directly into the spider's web. The fly's house was just around the corner and here he was stuck in the

trap of the dreadful, wicked spider. The fly struggled to get out of the entanglement, silently praying that the spider was asleep. His prayer went unanswered.

The spider spied the fly, and with a contented smile crawled towards her victim. It is only the tongue that can interpret a palatable meal, thought the spider as she moved towards the fly.

The fly struggled to go free, but fate and time were not on his side, as the spider moved towards him for the kill. The fly struggled, struggled, and struggled, but in vain...

Akoto woke up with a start, sweating as if he had been in a struggle. He felt a strong sensation of heat on his skin and got up to sit on his bed.

Akoto didn't remember the last time he had dreamt. Even if he did, he didn't remember the full plot when he woke up. His friend Kweku was the dreamer; he had a tale to tell each morning. You could be sure to hear another tale from him if he slept in the afternoon. Akoto teased him that his many dreams resulted directly from the sumptuous meals he ate each night before he slept, that and the fertile ground for constructing mischief, the ground he called his brain: Kweku the smart guy, Kweku the mischief, Kweku the fox.

However, this dream was so vividly etched on his memory. He tried to reflect on what the dream could mean; back home, a dream was supposed to be a premonition of a future occurrence and this one was interesting – with a spider, an Ananse.

Meanwhile, he was surprised Adoma hadn't written to him after the very first letter and that was in the first month he arrived. Thoughts of her filled his every minute when he was awake and he went to sleep each night reminiscing their days together. Beautiful, lovely, sweet Adoma. He was on track with his promise to return in a year and a half, and he was slaving away, doing odd jobs to accumulate funds. Anytime he bent down to clean the hospital floor, each time he was abused by some of his colleagues at the construction site where he worked on weekends, on the occasions he missed the bus and had to walk in the cold weather because he had to rush from lectures to the security job where he worked thrice a week on night shift, he thought about Adoma. He had bought most of the items needed for both the customary rites and the actual wedding. He had also prepared his attire for the two ceremonies. There was so much he needed to discuss with Adoma at that point – and so much to plan. Her silence puzzled him greatly.

The only letters he received from Ghana were from his buddy Kweku Ananse, and they did not convey good news. In one instance, Kweku reported that Adoma was the secret girlfriend of the chief of Wasa Asikuma. Kweku said after several chats with her to put a stop to the immoral affair, she still persisted. To Akoto's query why Adoma wasn't writing to him, Kweku asked him how someone who is busily enjoying a sumptuous meal would have time to talk. Yet Akoto didn't lose hope and continued to write, care of Ananse his trusted friend.

Kweku the banker was seriously enjoying the game, and the web he was spinning around Adoma and Akoto. He walked into his dedicated cabinet where he kept the letters of the two lovebirds. The cabinet was divided into two, with labels: Adoma and Akoto.

"Stupid Akoto! Such a fool" he laughed. "A foolish man in a pensive mood is making no judicious plan, he is still a buffoon," Kweku said aloud, falling to the floor in uncontrollable laughter.

November. Kweku decided that he had prepared the ground well enough. It was time to pluck the over-ripe coconut. He set off early that Friday and got to Asikuma just before dusk. Adoma's face lit when she saw him walking into her compound. After insisting that he took a bath, they sat to a meal of fufu and palmnut soup, with a good helping of bush meat and snails.

Later, seated in the verandah infront of her sitting room, the conversation soon turned to Akoto.

"Kweku, please can we discuss more pleasant issues?"

As it was said, fufu had fallen into soup! The iron was hot and it was time to hit it.

"Adoma, my Adoma, don't you think it is time to admit that someone else is showing you the love that your beauty deserves?"

"Ei, you Kweku and your roundabout way of speaking! Who could this be?"

"Adoma, Ama Adoma, look at me. Haven't I done enough to let you know that I love you? I have loved you from the very first time I saw you, but how could I tell you when you only had eyes for Akoto? Faithful as a friend can be, I have been supportive of my friend, but with this inexplicable behaviour, why should I continue to suppress my love? Marry me, Ama Adoma. I love you!"

Adoma's patience for Akoto had waned and she was angry as well. Akoto had treated her shabbily and she wanted to pay him back!

"Adoma, hold on, wait for your love; you know Akoto will not disappoint you, something must be wrong!" That inner voice again.

"No!" This time her mind took over. She willed for her heart to see reason with her mind. "I can't wait forever for him. Life is too short to be wasted on someone who takes his loved one for granted."

The tussle between heart and mind went on for months. She became stressed with this inner struggle. It showed in her blank face, devoid of that buoyant expression her pupils and colleagues alike loved.

Two years went by and still no news of Akoto reached her. Adoma finally gave in to the incessant pressure from Kweku. The wedding at the Holy Tabernacle of the Lord, the latest charismatic church in town, was planned and executed in record time. Kweku convinced Adoma that, knowing her family's preference for Akoto, it was not prudent to involve them. In any case, before anyone took the message to them in Dunkwa-on-Offin, the wedding would have been over and the deal sealed. With the certificate of notice from the local authorities, they approached the church and had the quiet wedding.

Kweku had won the target of two years and he felt so satisfied. In a little over a month, he was ready to move on to his new target. He had trapped the crab and not the water in it. The water could flow away for all he cared!

In December, three years after Akoto had travelled and more than a year later than he had promised to come back, he returned to Ghana. He had used his time abroad to study part-time for his law degree. He was so excited on his flight back home. He had not been faithful to his promise, but he was sure Adoma would understand. Especially when he had written to both Adoma herself and Kweku (so he could add his voice to his plea), explaining his delay. Now, he was going to marry the love of his youth. Not hearing from Adoma all these years heightened his excitement further.

On arrival, he went straight to Kweku's home and that was where he crashed down to earth! His love, the object of his attention, the reason for his almost slave-like toil in a foreign land, the lady of his heart had been married in his absence and to the one person he trusted above all, save God!

He rushed from Kweku's house, went straight back home and wept. Between his bouts of sobs, he spoke to his empty room.

"Ah Kweku! *Ah ah ah*! If anyone would do this to me, it shouldn't have been you! Why did you have to prove our elders right that the ant that will bite you is in your own cloth, *eh*?"

He couldn't forget the smile of victory on Kweku's face as he left his friend's house. Finally, it was this image of his smiling friend that stopped his copious tears. Did the elders not say that one could not weep and meditate at the same time? Akoto decided to do all he could to wipe away that grin, nay smirk, from the face of the scoundrel. He decided to win back his love. Kweku had eaten his yam and Akoto was determined to let him choke on it. His father's words came to him: that if a snake came out of a hole and invited you to dip your hand into the same, there was nothing to be afraid of because the danger in that hole was already out. Kweku's trickery and strategy were already out and Akoto knew he could beat him at his own game.

The next day, he went to the school where Adoma was teaching. She had been transferred to Accra following her marriage. The reunion between the two was frosty at first. At break time, Akoto was able to pull her away from her class to a quiet restaurant.

"Adoma, why? Why didn't you wait for me? Why?" Akoto was holding back tears.
"*Eh*, please hold on. See the black pot calling the kettle black! I should rather be asking you why you disappointed me so. Why you did not get

in touch with me for so long? Why you did not reply my letters? Why you did not bother to write to me? Did you think for once that I am a human being, a woman with feelings?" Adoma let down the dam that held all her hurts, mixed with regrets.

"Are you telling me you never received the many letters I sent to you through Kweku? Even though you had written to me only once? Even when I was informed you were not being faithful to me!"

"Whaaat!! Me being unfaithful to you? You wrote to me through Kweku?"

"Yes, Adoma. I have always written, sharing all my experiences, and also explaining why I had to spend more time to complete my law studies. And I even wrote the latest last month, informing you I was coming back in December. Did you not receive that too?"

"Oh, Jesus!" That was all Adoma could say. She broke down and wept.

It became obvious to both of them that Kweku had played them apart, to his benefit.

"Adoma, I still love you and you know that. I know you still love me, and that would not change."

"Akoto, I do know you love me and I still do love you, but I am married to your friend, that cheat!"

They affirmed their love to each other and pledged to find a way to pay Kweku back in his own coin.

When Adoma told Akoto later that the customary rites were not even performed, Akoto knew he had Kweku by the scruff! Legally, the notice for marriage from the local authorities was valid only on the basis that customary marriage had been done. And also, the pastor of the church where the wedding was held had not been licensed by the municipal authority to perform marriages! Therefore, the marriage between Adoma and Kweku was null and void! The fact that Akoto was a lawyer played no small part in the investigations! Indeed, knowledge of the law had triumphed over trickery!

Trouble, it is said, is like a storm: it doesn't rain; it pours. Just about the same time that Kweku's marriage to Adoma was annulled, an audit at the Accra International Bank, where Kweku worked, revealed a serious scandal which Kweku was involved in.

But it is dangerous to under-estimate the cunning of a man such like Kweku Ananse, son of Owawani Ananse, for a man who built a house of lies usually equipped it with a large window through which to escape when he got into trouble. Before the police could lay their hands on Ananse, he had bolted. He lived by the adage of the jungle that it was better to escape with shots and injury, than to be captured for the fire. Besides Kweku was in no mood for the prison.

The wedding of Adoma and Akoto was held in grand style at the Holy Ghost Cathedral, with the heads of the Orthodox churches in attendance. As for Kweku, Adoma and Akoto thought he had his due recompense. Why should the chicken weep and fast in sympathy for a hawk which is imprisoned? In their joy, they had no tears for Ananse, no.

Adoma and Akoto can be seen on the streets of Accra, living happily!

DRIBBLE DE ZAGIDIBOGIDI

"He who moulds your head (like a waterpot) is the one who can break it." Akan proverb

He bore his rage calmly as he sat at the back of the taxi. *C'mon, control. You are nearly there.* He tumbled at the knife in his bag. It was razor-sharp, just the right condition he needed for the job at hand. This dish needed to be served cold. It tasted sweetest when served cold. Payback.

What a boyish face. He looked at the new guy who was to join him and Abondi in their room. The two of them had been very good friends since secondary school and had booked the same room for their second year in the University. One student had to join to complete the number of students assigned to each room, and he was quite sure they could cope with this babyface.

"Whassya name boy?"
"Robert, but my friends call me Robbie."
"Well then, may I call you Robbie."
It was not a request, more like a statement.

He decided that he liked the guy. He could stay. If he had decided otherwise, the boy would have been booted out, one way or the other. Everyone knew that Hardened, aka Zagidibogidi, had his own way in every thing. His father's fame played no little part.

He hated traffic jams. They had a way of occurring when he was in a hurry. Almost always. Particularly today when he wished the taxi could fly. And the weather was hot too. Damn.

They got on well with Babyface. The boy was pure innocence. Whilst he and Abondi were into all the fun campus had to offer, Babyface was all about righteousness and holy holy. The Jesus way and all that.

73

Why at all had he boarded this rickety old taxi? The driver had parked near the police station on the Liberation Road and was fidgeting with his engine. Didn't he know that this was Get Even Day? Well, would he care?

Rose. His rose. The charming sweet figure of a lady who was the toast of all on the campus. It had taken a long full year to woo her. The many notes, love notes he had written. Not counting the payment of the small boys who acted as courier agents. The visits that occupied a non-negotiable place in his daily routine. The pain of her continual rejection that nearly paralyzed his heart. The hurt to his pride. All his life, he had gotten what he wanted. The blow to his ego. The longing to be linked to her name that became an obsession.

Eventually. Didn't Babyface mouth that aphorism - there is a time for everything? He had always known, too, there was time for nothing. Was he called Hardened for nothing's sake? He had a crocodile skin. Even the hardest bone succumbed to the teeth of the patient dog. He pestered her. He followed her. He flattered her. He spoilt her with gifts. She could no longer pretend that he didn't exist. Or didn't care.

She gave in. Eventually. One long year of perseverance. And not letting go. Never. She was his Rose. Of Sharon, to borrow one of Babyface's.

His friends on his floor carried him shoulder-high on the day of his conquest. Straight into the pond. They rejoiced with him. Rose was all he needed to be what he really was to be. She changed his life. Bye-bye to the Guy called Hardened, the Zagidi. Enter Randy Sandin. He started taking life seriously, for a change. Thanks to his Rose. Monkey no fine, but if his mother continues to love him, Monkey could at least start bathing. Walking well. Speaking well. Zagidi changed, for his Rose' sake.

The taxi was moving again, at last. A mechanic had to come and help. He had no choice but to wait since he couldn't afford to pay for truncating the journey and a change in transportation. The taxi drivers didn't charge the same fare from station to station when that distance was covered in two taxi journeys. He had waited for years, a few minutes wouldn't hurt. He looked at the clock on the taxi's dashboard; they had about twenty more minutes of travelling to do. He thought about how he would do it. He may allow him to do a little talking. You know, like in the movies. A little Confession before the hood falls. Not good to meet the Old Man upstairs with unacknowledged sin all over. The second part of the Judgement, he would give the Old Man the privilege of executing. The first act was his for the taking. Exclusively his.

The news had shocked him. Someone had tampered with his Rose. Desecrated his temple, his object of worship. He heard it in the lecture room. Raped the previous night, after he had visited her. Her room-mates had travelled and he had kept her company. They had conversed a lot, on a broad range of topics. About their future, together. Their future home. Their future kids. Their future this. Their future that. He had left her waving at the junction to her hall. Waving and smiling. Late in the night. She never got back to her room.

He quickly rushed to the Hospital. At the Entrance, he was stopped by a grim-faced policeman, who flashed an ID at him and escorted him to the waiting van.

Everything happened so fast. He lost track of time.

Rose had been raped. Fact.
He had been arrested and was awaiting trial. Fact.
He didn't know why. Fact.

At the trial, he saw them. His friends in the University. No pity in those eyes. Their message came piercing his heart.

Rapist!

He couldn't stand the glare. He squirmed under the force of their ocular judgement and feared and loathed it more than the verdict of the jury.

When the verdict finally came, he was not surprised. He had pleaded not guilty, but who would take him seriously after his fame on campus, for his way with women, for his violent ways.

But Rose changed that! He wanted to scream.

Not to be believed. Added to that, he was the last person seen with her.

His parents had also been in court, on the date of the verdict. Only that day. They did not believe him. They sent a note through the lawyer who elected to defend him, pro bono. He should consider himself no more a part of the Sandins. He was the black sheep of the family. He had brought disgrace to the mighty name.

Only his Rose could tell the truth, she who trusted him but alas, she lay in intensive care, in coma.

Kong!

The sharp rap of the Judge's mallet snapped him out of his reverie.

He was sentenced to twenty years imprisonment, with hard labour. There was general agreement in the courtroom. Hugs and pats. The Monster was to be put away. He wished his beloved Rose was out of coma to testify his innocence.

77

They were now on the 6th Avenue road. His target's office was on the Fourth Close off that road. He felt the weapon once again. Should it be a slit throat or a stab? In the back? Perhaps in the heart. Where it hurts most. After all, had he not stabbed him in the heart too? Where it had hurt him real bad.

Abondi had visited him in prison a few weeks after the sentencing. Babyface didn't come till much later. Only once, because he decided not to see Babyface again, not after what Abondi told him.

It felt eerie the first time he had a visitor – Abondi. The prison officer could as well have sat at the table with them, he stood so close.

"Zagidi, Charlie sorry man! We know say no be you do am! Why? Life be so unfair!" Zagidi could feel the pain in Abondi's voice. His close pal of many years, his shame was Abondi's as well.

Then he dropped the bombshell.

It was Babyface who had implicated Zagidi. Babyface had sworn he had seen him at midnight with about three boys he couldn't recognize, and that this gang raped Rose. Babyface had identified a shirt that was found at the scene of the crime as Randy's. This was the shirt that had been tendered as the main exhibit in court, the main basis upon which he was arrested, charged and convicted.

He had planned his revenge since then. He had been determined each passing day of toil and untold hardship, all undeserved. Now the time had come. Finally, it had come.

After four years, he had been released. He hadn't bothered to find out why and how he had been released early. Not his bother. Find and kill, that was his bother.

It had taken only two days to trace Babyface. A successful lawyer. "Well, your days are numbered, Baby Boy. I am seeing to the First Part of the Judgement", Randy thought.

The taxi screened to a halt. Zagidi nearly missed the office and had to bark at the taxi driver to stop. His voice and his mask of anger must have frightened the driver. Randy alighted and looked up the signpost in front of the building. Winner Chambers. He chuckled.

A couple of minutes later, he was in Robert Handleman's office. Babyface hadn't changed much. The lawyer looked up, studied the visitor's face, took in the unkempt beard, bloodshot eyes and recognition dawned.

"Randy! Hey, Randy! It's you! Praise God! At last you are free and you are here!"

For a fleeting moment, Hardened wrestled with the murderous feelings that yearned for released. What guts! "You send me to prison and you sound like Holy Mary!"

"Cut it man! Cut it!" he thundered, with enough anger to bring a cup of iced water to boiling point. "Praise my foot! I do the talking and I assure you, it shall not be long. Shall be as short as this."

He recovered his composure, went to the door, locked it and put the key in his pocket.

Calmly he brought out the weapon and thoughtfully turned it over in his hand. The blade glinted. He sat down in the chair and looked at the lawyer. How he hated him. The lawyer was uneasy, Zagidi was enjoying it.

"Don't even dare!" Babyface's hand was suspended over the telephone.

"Now! You want to confess. Before you die? Hurry!"

So he didn't know, thought Robbie, as he looked up at his former room-mate and felt sorry for him.

"You think I caused your imprisonment?" *Good God! This lawyer Babyface wasn't just stupid, he was naïve too. Who did it?*
"Randy, Abondi caused your fall." *What! You must be joking. Abondi my buddy buddy?*
"It is all here, my friend. Here in these papers. Abondi signed this affidavit before he died. He raped Rose. Together with his friends. He always wanted her but you got her first." *Stop it! Stop it! Stop it, man! I can't bear it anymore. I caaaan't!*
"It was on the strength of this evidence that you were released. I arranged your release. I couldn't come to tell you myself since I found out that you didn't want to see me. Welcome home, man. It is all over. The nightmare is over."

Randy started weeping like a child. How could Robbie be so nice when he had wanted so much to kill him? Did he also know that Abondi had lied about him?

"And Rose? What happened to her?" Randy asked, after calming down.
"Randy, God has been good again. Rose was flown out of Ghana overseas, where she recently regained her full sense of speech after many years of therapy. She returned to Ghana only a few months ago. Would you like to see her?"

Three hours later, a new Randy, in new clothes Robbie had bought for him that day started feeling invigorated after a good bath and meal. He sat near Rose on a couch in her father's living room and held her hand. Robbie smiled at them. They will be together again.

"Randy, let bygones be bygones, OK."
Hardened softened. His tongue was not used to this exercise. "Can you forgive me, Robbie?"
"Of course, I can." "I must."
"But why? How can you?"

Robbie smiled. "The Jesus Way, remember?"

HOPE UNDEFERRED

Dear Kwesi,

This letter comes with a reminder of the best gift I can ever give to anyone - my heart, my love, my life. It is very late here but I am very much awake, 'cos my dear, you are on my mind. Always on my mind. Cupid sent his arrow my way and I lurched forward with my bosom once I espied your name on the tail of the arrow; come and see the hole it has created in my heart. What sweet pain! I have heard one say that love, like a flower, quickly blooms and attracts but with the same celerity evaporates like a mirage in the Kalahari. If that is a popular opinion I walk a lonely path then, because my love for you is like the seed that forms in a woman's womb - once fertilised, it only knows growth. Like a mixture of concrete, this love hardens and intensifies in strength as it walks hand in hand with time.

Ah! my heart bleeds with this wound of love. I want you to walk this path of ecstasy, this journey of bliss, this adventure of forever-ness with me - always. I miss you terribly, so much my dear. Come quickly, my Prince, and heal my wound, my heart aches for you, my soul yearns for you and my eyes long to set their gaze on you, again.

I want to sing it out, shout it, tell it on the mountain tops to anyone who cares to listen, to the birds so they carry it to the ends of the world - you are mine, and oh, I love you. Lemme hear from you, darling, because you are all I live for.
She who is yours,
Rabbs

*S*he sat back and looked at the letter again. The words seemed to connect with her very soul and as she focused on each line of the letter, she seemed to be imbuing the words with her spirit, to carry exactly the emotions she felt to the intended recipient. The words seemed to her more poetry than prose, poetry both sad and meaningful, poignant, full of life, and she was hoping that these words will be her angels of plea to bring her relief from the pain of love. It was about 1 a.m. and the night was as quiet as a stillborn baby. She did not attempt to hold back the tears that overflowed the swollen banks of her eyes, coursing down her cheeks and finding their way into her mouth like River Ankobra's journey to the Atlantic ocean. The salty taste did nothing to soothe her aching heart. Her portable stereo oozed Kojo Antwi's song *Dade anoma* [Metal bird, a reference to an aeroplane], connecting with the thoughts she had transmitted onto paper. She wished, in tandem with the Musicman, that a bird would suddenly appear to take her letter to her loved one. She clutched the paper to her breast, rose and walked to the window, slowly, and watched through the netting. The serenity outside contrasted sharply with her own feelings, the cool breeze caressing her plump wet cheeks.

Kwesi was two years ahead of her in the secondary school, Amenfiman High. Araba knew him as a very serious science student, who was so much in love with his books. Rarely did you see him on campus without a book - a textbook, a novel - a book nevertheless. He wore a grave countenance most of the time. He also had an aura of pensiveness about him. Even in the dining hall, where it was usual for students to chit-chat and tease each other especially before meals, Kwesi would sit quietly at table, reading while meals were being served, eating without as much as a look around him. In Amenfiman, there were five houses each for the boys and girls. The houses were named such that there were five pairs. It was the custom that the girls in the female houses shared tables with the occupants of the counterpart male houses. Kwesi was in Bassanyin House, whose counterpart female house was Akoaa house; providence collaborated with fate to ensure Araba and Kwesi shared the same table. She admired him but only at a distance. He was so sober, how could anyone get across to such? He seemed quite content being by himself at all times, self-contained, not caring for a chat. The impression was that he would not even have time for anyone, let alone maintaining a friendship with the opposite sex.

She overhead the conversation at the corner of Akoaa dormitory called *nnipa nse hwee*, translated loosely as 'man is worthless', as she passed on her way to the bathroom for her afternoon bath. Nnipa nse hwee (NNH) was the gossip headquarters of the school and being the topic for discussion at NNH was of two-fold significance: the subject was important and the worth of the subject after an NNH treatment was less than that of an orphanage dog.

"That Kwesi boy, who does he think he is?" That was Enyonam, *Kokonsa hemaa* (queen of gossip).
"Which Kwesi are you girls talking about? I hope it is not my Kwesi o!"

Lady Tinash was just returning to the dormitory from class; she didn't normally patronize lunch in the dining hall, as she considered it beneath her status as a leading lady in the school. She delved straight into the gossip.

"Tinash, ah, you know your Kwesi cannot be discussed here; you know when we talk about him, it is only in flowery terms!" Sexy Gogormi was the moderator for this particular topic; indeed, she was like the communications and information director of Nnipa Nse Hwee, bringing in topical issues for deliberation.

Enyonam continued, "It is the Mills-Brown guy, because he thinks he is handsome and intelligent, he goes around strutting like a Manhyia[2] peacock, thinking of himself better than everyone else."

"Who says he is handsome?"

"Ebei, *SG* (her friends called Gogormi by the abbreviated form of her nickname), don't act like the hunter who said the bird wasn't nice afterall, when he failed to shoot it after stalking it for days. Aren't you the same gal who used to fancy Mills-Brown?"

All the girls burst out laughing. Tinash was like that. With her choice Asante proverbs, she could bring humor into the discussions and also cut right to the bone. When she wanted to be caustic in her remarks, those same proverbs came in handy.

"But seriously, girls, does that boy fear girls or what? I was on the same table with him last year, he was so shy of us!"

"I don't think it is shyness, it is pride!" SG insisted.

"But he is an SU (Scripture union) member, how can he be proud?"

"*Kai*," SG exploded scornfully, "their pride is even worse, when it is covered by a false spiritual cloak."

Hmm, it was a fearful thing to fall into the hands of the NNH council. Interestingly, though, the more the girls discussed Kwesi, the more Araba thought of him; she just could not get him off her mind. She was beginning to understand that Kwesi's apparent aloofness was a challenge to many and this situation to her was like wind to fire - it extinguished the small and rekindled the mighty.

The Scripture union (SU) brought most young christians on campus together; both Araba and Kwesi were members. One evening at SU, the program was *Interaction time*, during which members were supposed to

[2]Manhyia Palace is the official residence of the Asante King.

interact with and get to know one another better. After a short time of prayer and singing, the MC for the evening asked members to chat amongst themselves. Araba turned to find the first person to talk to, and who did she face but Kwesi! Kwesi, of all the people at the meeting! Her heart missed a beat, no, two beats!

"Hello, I am Kwesi Mills-Brown, Form 5 Science," he opened up.
"Hi, my name is Araba...Araba Frimpomaa Larbi. Three C."

The ice was broken. They talked exclusively the entire period, a duration which most used to chat with about three persons altogether. It was a hilarious chat they had. It was as if they had known each other for years. She was pleasantly surprised by his sense of humor. Indeed, appearances are deceptive, but smell is not. Had the elders not said that it is only when you shake the neem tree that you smelt it well? Definitely one needed to get closer to be able to shake - you can't shake by remote control. She was struck by his quiet nature, his simple choice of words and his depth of knowledge. After exchanging basic information about each other - age, subjects offered, favorite food etc - interspersed with jokes and anecdotes, Kwesi challenged her to live for the Lord and never give up her faith, in whatever difficulty she went through; to value her salvation, since it was the best thing that had and would ever happen to her.

Before long, it was time for the meeting to wind up and Araba and Kwesi had to go back to their seats. He again expressed his pleasure at meeting her and promised to keep in touch.

Araba took a long time sleeping that night. She was excited. She replayed the conversation they had in her mind the umpteenth time. Oh, Kwesi was so pleasant to talk to. Truly, you could not judge an object from afar, she philosophised. She resolved to know him better, for here surely was a friend worth keeping. She reasoned that it was not that Kwesi felt superior to others but that he was just not an extrovert. Only when you got close to such people did you find the gold in them. *Eh, Araba, are you now a psychologist*, she teased her thoughts, with a laugh. With a beatific smile on her face, she drifted into a peaceful sleep, embracing her thoughts and taking a stroll into dreamland.

True to his word, Kwesi sent a note to her the next morning.

> *Hi Rabbs, [Oh he remembered! Araba smiled at his reference to her nickname]*
>
> *It was great chatting with you yesterday. Once again, it's been a pleasure meeting you. I hope to be a friend, and a good one too. There are a lot of things we can share together - our challenges, our anxieties, and of course God's word. Keep on keeping on in the Lord.*
>
> *God bless,*
> *Kwesi*

That note opened the gates to a fulfilling friendship between them. Kwesi and Araba kept nothing hidden from each other, encouraging and spurring one another on. They became an epitome of friendship on campus and grew fond of each other each passing day.

Time flew quickly, but the bonds of friendship remained and deepened. A lot happened. Kwesi passed his 'O' Levels and continued at the same school. After his statutory National service, he continued to the University. He was in his fourth year in Medical school when Araba wrote the letter, that memorable letter, to him.

Araba was teaching for her National service at Assin Kabrofo after completing Teachers' Training College. Her friendship with Kwesi had developed into something stronger, that 'something' Araba found out during this period of her service.

The National service in faraway Assin, about four hundred kilometers from the capital city, was taking its toll on Araba. Her job as a teacher in the local junior secondary school was exhausting. She was miles away from home, in the midst of unfamiliar people; she felt so lonely. Her companions were the many letters that came from Kwesi, she looked forward to them each week with the expectation of a pregnant woman in her ninth month. Kwesi had become her pillar, a great companion, a balm that soothed her in times of depression and frustration. It was in the dense forest area of Assin, where her loneliness lead her to do extensive reflections - excursions in her mind she called them, that she came to the realization that she was indeed in love. In love and with Kwesi. She saw him, now, not only as a friend and a brother, but a life companion. In retrospect and with the benefit of maturity, she understood her initial feelings towards Kwesi now - it was a seed of affectionate love, right from the start.

But for two months now, she hadn't heard from Kwesi. Had Kwesi deserted her, discarded her, left her when she needed him most, when her mind had finally accepted what her heart has been belting out for a long time, that she was in love with him? Had her love been in vain? She had heard many stories about those University guys, how they could easily forget about their steadies as soon as they feasted their eyes on those *kyingilingi*[3] Varsity girls. *You can't do this to me, Kwesi, surely you can't*...but did he love her too, she asked herself yet again. "Never assume a man's love", she reminded herself. What if Kwesi just saw her as a sister in Christ, a friend?

Ebo Nkwantabisa was known far and wide in the Assin area. A famed hunter, it was believed that if one held a finger up, Ebo could shoot it off at a hundred yards. The antelope and the duiker he had killed, the black-and-white colobus and the warthog he had subdued. He also loved to hunt other species in the land of the living: girls - nubile young women. He had a similar reputation in that enterprise as well.

When he set his eyes on the new teacher of A1, one of the two local L.A. Middle School (even though the educational system had moved to the Junior Secondary School naming, the old name still stuck in the local lingua), his adrenalin level shot up a thousand notches. In the game of winning ladies, he operated the same strategy he employs in the thick of the forest: study the intended target (likes, dislikes, sounds), observe its daily routine, draw a line of approach (including baits, traps), lie in wait patiently and strike opportunistically. Needless to say, his success rate was high and it helped that he was the chief's son.

Araba usually woke up at 5.30 each morning, to say her daily prayers and read the Bible, before opening her door. As a teacher, she didn't have to go to the Ankobra river to fetch water. The headmaster had a roster for the pupils to supply each teacher with water, firewood and/or charcoal. Water, the pupils procured from the river. Firewood and charcoal, they supplied as non-syllabus items under *Arts & Craft*. With this blanket subject, sundry items were provided by the pupils at no extra cost to the school.

Araba's foot hit an item, in a sack, on the ground as she stepped out of her room. It was a bit foggy, as the monsoon and harmattan winds had started spreading a haze across the countryside. She jumped back immediately, a bit frightened. She went back into her room and waited for the day to fully break.

She called out for Baffour, a boy in the house, to come and help her open the sack. Inside the sack was a roasted grass-cutter, its limbs linked by arrow-like sticks, spread-eagle.

"Baffour Maame!"
"Yes, Miss, *maa kye* (good morning)."

The village folk called every female teacher Miss, whether married or single. Araba lived in a *compound house*, of five families, each occupying a unit of two rooms. The entire compound house shared one bathroom, and for nature's call, the newly commissioned communal *KVIP* was the place to go. It was Baffour Maame's turn to sweep the courtyard. As a privilege, again, Araba was exempt from sweeping the courtyard or scrubbing the bathroom. *Bush allowance* for teachers, it was called.

"Auntie, please, did you see the person who brought this?"

Auntie Edufa smiled to herself. She knew only one person who used that strategy in Kabrofo.

"No, I didn't see anyone drop it there. I was up when the first cock crowed but no one has come near your door."
"Hmm. OK, can you please keep this on the top of your barn for me, so it still gets smoked? I need to find out who brought it before I do anything with it."

After school that day, Araba crossed the school field from A1 towards the street that separated Old Town from Sikafuo Amantem. She took the path behind Opanyin Apusika's shop, and turned left into the market. She needed to buy some dried fish for the kontomire stew she was planning to cook. Baffour Maame had given her gift of ten well-built fingers of plantain and she intended to do justice to them.

With her fish and *kontomire*[4] duly bought, Araba went by Nana Potisaa's house to say hi to the old lady. Madam Potisaa was one of the oldest in the village and particularly liked Araba, saying she resembled her long deceased grand-daughter. Araba gave the old lady the two tins of sardine she always took to her and sat by her bed to chat for a while.

Kwame Atta, one of Nana Potisaa's grandchildren, came in.

"Miss, Bra Ebo is looking for you." She didn't know anyone by that name, but Kwame sounded excited. Araba stepped out to see a tall, well-built man sitting on the veranda.

He got up and extended his hand; she shook it.

"Please, did you get the *akrantie*[5] I asked Atta to bring to you yesterday?"
Mystery solved.

"Yes, I did. I didn't know who it was from though."
"Ah, oh, it was from me. I trapped it myself and dried it in a special way, just for you, Miss.
"Thank you, but I don't eat *bush meat*."
"Oh."

It has been a particularly tiring day. It was about 4.30 p.m. and she had just returned from school after preparing her students for the impending examinations. Getting home was becoming a chore too – she had to watch out for Ebo, changing routes so she didn't have to cross paths with him. He had become more than a pest; perhaps

[4] Cocoyam leaves used in a vegetable stew.
[5] Grasscutter.

unable to realize that not all girls were his for the taking in the village. His gifts had progressed from bush meat through mutton to kente, all in a bid to win her. Baffour Maame's soup had undergone a revolutionary upgrade since Ebo set his heart on Araba. Not hearing from Kwesi exacerbated her frustration at the situation.

It had been a week since she mailed that letter to Kwesi. As she changed into her housedress, to try and relax in bed, her thoughts turned to him almost automatically, immediately, effortlessly.

A knock on the door. Who should be disturbing my limited peace of mind at this time of day, she wasn't pleased to wonder. She hesitated for a moment, but the knocking persisted. Sometimes her neighbours, especially Baffour Maame, could be tenacious when they wanted to ask her opinion on an issue. Again, what if it was Ebo Nkwantabisa? Her heart missed a beat.

"Not him, Lord!" she prayed. She rose and opened the door, reluctantly.

"Kwesi!"

She leapt into his arms. He nearly lost his footing; she was besides herself with joy. Kwesi smiled at her, that slow delicious smile of his that melted her innards. She didn't relax her embrace, and he practically had to carry her to the sofa. Araba looked up at him in sheer wonderment, it was so good to be true, Kwesi with her and such a swift answer to her prayers! Such a speedy response to her letter, far beyond her expectations, really!

He suggested they go out for a walk. She obliged and soon with her arms intertwined into his, they took the path that went towards Moseaso, by the peaceful flowing waters of the Ankobra, the waters

lovingly washing the rocks in an intricate, ancient ritual, undisturbed by the passage of time. For some time, they walked in silence. Interesting, reflected Araba, that silence could be so enjoyable when it was shared with someone significant, that silence could speak when one was well tuned to its frequency, when the ambience was right. Araba revelled in the moment and wished it would not end.

Kwesi broke the silence eventually, with a squeeze of Araba's hand. He explained why he had not written for such a long time. He had been on a team of medical students' outreach to the Brong Ahafo region to educate the folks on malaria prevention, as part of a UN-sponsored project. They had been away for about two months and on their return, he found Araba's letter in his pigeonhole - he came to Assin immediately.

"Oh Kwesi" was all Araba could say. She felt cherished, and all the anxiety and tension in the past couple of months seemed to ebb and dissipate.

They were now on the outskirts of the village, on the southern part. The sun was beginning his journey to his sleeping abode, and most of the villagers were returning to their homes from the day's work at their farms, with loads of foodstuff and firewood on their heads. Araba waved back at Auntie Mansa, who had her sixth child tired to her back, with two of her children following their father, who held in his hands a freshly trapped grasscutter. A visitor of *Miss* was always welcome and many of the other folks smiled, waved or stopped to shake hands. It was better to shake hands, since a wave from afar was sometimes deemed uncouth and referred to as cutting a branch of a tree! However, few stopped to shake the hands of the visitor, as they sensed that Miss wanted some privacy.

Kwesi turned Araba to face him and he looked down into her eyes.

"My dear, know this. We may still have a long way to go but take this from me. Allow me to borrow from Scripture. Human as I am, I promise never to leave you or forsake you. You seem to think you alone have the capacity to love, more than all men; all ladies have that false impression. Hear this: I love you back! So long have I loved you, and I have had to admit it to myself, eventually. I know I haven't shown it much, I needed to be careful, to be sure of myself, of my commitment, to move appreciation to affection. But now I know that my love is for you, and I want to shout it out too, now!"

He embraced Araba warmly. Contentment showed on both faces as they remained in their embrace. Far above them, the sun smiled gently on the two lovebirds and shone his blessings on them, as he opened the door to his house. The songs of the birds ceased, the wind quietened, the tree branches craned their long necks, all nature seemed to come to a standstill as Kwesi and Araba walked back to the village slowly, arms linked, down the aisle of life, a solemn procession with nature as their companion and audience, back to the village, back to love, back to peace. Heartaches may still come their way but, at least, they knew they had a cure - their love.

KOJO NKRABEAH

It was still dark, but I knew it was about 3 a.m. Not that I had a watch - no, I had learnt to tell the time from the skies and the sounds around. I had been awoken by one of those giant mosquitoes who looked so gigantic you'd think they had been reared. Their breeding ground was only a few metres from my bedfloor, the gutters whose waters were so dark one could be tempted to believe the colour of water is black. I saw, nay heard, another mosquito coming towards me. I still couldn't decide which I loathed the most – the mosquitoes' bite or the irritating sound they made as they flew past my ears. I drove the mosquito away with my three-months-no-touch-water sleeping cloth, and with all the force that my feeble arm could muster.

I turned to look at my fellow inhabitants of that floor of residence, each sleeping on his bed. Did I say bed? Actually, they were sleeping on mats or, to be precise, clothes that had dual purposes – worn during the day and slept on during the night. I was no exception. I really envied those who could sleep so soundly in that environment. They seemed to have developed impermeable rubber skins, at least with respect to the proboscis of the sucking insect. These skins appear immune to cold, heat, ants and a myriad of harsh conditions. Pure adaptations, I reasoned.

I sat up straight and scratched my body. The city was still very much asleep, but sleep had eluded me. I stood up, stretched and yawned. 'Hmm, what fatigue.' You couldn't sleep on a cloth, on such a floor and expect to feel like a king when you woke up. My body was aching real bad, as if I had been given a good thrashing. I walked to our backyard and washed my mouth and face. A chewing stick quickly found its way into my mouth. As I chewed, sitting on my cloth-turned-mat, recapping my life and how I ended up in that place was almost automatic…

101

I really missed Moseaso, that quiet village where I was born; well, that is where I grew up to find myself. I found myself living with a family of six, including the parents, and, of course, excluding me. Because I was the outsider. No one needed to tell me, I realized that myself. Kojo Nkrabeah was the name I responded to.

Village folks! They are always ready to tell you what you always wanted to know, even when you had not asked for any such information. Maame Akyea was particularly good at that; it was her talent, her gift. She, it was, who told me about my parents, my siblings, and how I ended up in Opanyin Akrumah's house.

She told me my parents had lived in Moseaso and had two other children apart from me. Opanyin Akrumah had been my Dad's bosom friend and both were farmers. Maame Akyea even showed me the location of my Dad's farm, which farm was then being managed by the Abusua. Her story had it that my parents had travelled to Dadieso with my older siblings for a funeral and to visit some relatives. I had been left behind with my cousin and Nanaa, my grandmother who was then visiting. On their way back, the *w'ato nkyene* they were travelling on was involved in an accident. None of the passengers survived. My parents and siblings extinguished by one act of fate. I was about two years then, the old woman added. Naana collapsed upon hearing the tragic news; she didn't live long after that.

My extended family, I was told, took over everything my hardworking parents had toiled to own, everything except me. The farms, the houses, everything. I was sent to live with my maternal Grandma. I nearly forgot to add this piece of classified information Maame Akyea whispered into my ears, telling me not to tell any one. "Please don't repeat it to anyone else," she pleaded. She said the whole village believed, and she the strongest, that it was Opanyin Akrumah who killed my father, that the accident was not natural. She said they suspected Opanyin Akrumah did so because my Dad posed a threat to him as he (my Dad) was becoming influential in the village, and Opanyin Akrumah was one who couldn't countenance the sight of anyone as powerful as he was, or becoming so. He really loved power, absolute power.

After my grandma's death, when I was about five years of age, I was sent to live with Opanyin Akrumah, partly because he wanted to give the impression that he loved my father so much so as to take his only child. Another reason, and my most plausible, really, was that no one else would have anything to do with me. Did the elders not say that it is only the son of a living king who could call himself a prince?

My life in that house was an endless chain of hardships. As far as I could remember, no one showed me an iota of love. That led me to suspect I wasn't a son of the house; Eno Akyea's story confirmed my fears. I was made to do every donkor[6] job in the house. "Nkrabeaaaaaah!!" and I must respond with the speed of the lightning that struck the coconut tree near Papa Mersu's house during the great rain, else a beating became my portion.

The children of the house lived like royals. Even the children treated me like trash ; especially Adadewaa, who was two years older than I was, the eldest of them all. She didn't even know how to cook, *tweah!* Their mother was worse, I feared her. She was always quick to remind me that I was a public liability, that but for their benevolence, I would have been long dead. Well, it no doubt was kind of them to take me into their home, but it certainly was an act of kindness that had to be paid for, in currency of suffering, toil and torture. I knew no happiness, no joy, just a monotone of desolation. The only oasis in the unending desert of bleakness were the times I spent at school and the evenings I managed to sneak from the house to Eno Akyea's house for stories about my family. How I enjoyed those stories, they were more enjoyable than the Ananse stories I heard. I used to dream about my lost family a lot. I dreamt of a peaceful home, loving parents and siblings...

"Kojo...Kay darling. How do you feel this morning?"
"I feel great, Mama."
"Come over and let me whisper something into your ears."
"Ei, Mama, what is it? Please tell me now, pleaassse!"

Tickle, tickle.

"Hehe, Mama, don't do that oo, haha."
"Guess what Kay...I have a surprise for you! Dada has just brought you a brand new bicycle!"
"Wow!"
"That's not all! For your birthday, he is taking you to Accra, the big city! Oh Kay, Happy birthday!"

One thing no one had the power to take away from me was my freedom to dream, but the keys to bring those wonderful scenes and conditions in my daily dreams into reality were locked away. It was a sequence. Dream, be happy, think it is real and boom! – back to reality.

"Nkrabeah, where did you put the shoes I asked you to polish?"
"I put them in your bedroom."
"What! Who gave you permission to enter my bedroom?"
"You asked me to take them there when I am done."
"Stupid boy! Who said you could enter my room with your dirty, smelly

body!"

I hated Adadewaa with all my heart. I feared her, because she was capable of concocting stories like a skilled village gossip, stories that her parents believed, so real yet so fictitious. Each of those stories either got me into trouble or extricated her from her many escapades. She was just like her mother. She was a spoilt, lazy girl; never wanting to do anything for herself, sending me on useless errands. My greatest dream then was to beat her up mercilessly. Until I could run away from the village, I dared not. I swallowed my hurt, and her nonsense, and waited for that time to come.

The city was waking up. I could smell the aroma of Sulley Maame's *waakye*[7]. It was a characteristic smell, and each of the boys could distil it even when twenty cooks were all cooking waakye at the same time. And each of us also knew that the aroma and the actual taste of Sulley Maame's waakye never converged. It was a standing joke that all the goodness of the waakye escaped in the aroma that got to us. You paid for the aroma, and not the taste. The aroma promised heaven and delivered, okay not hell, but close to that.

Yet every morning, we jostled for space to buy the waakye. It was cheap and we were allowed to sign the wall; that is, buy on credit. For trusted clients, Sulley Maame had a book in which she put a slash against the client's name for each day you bought on credit, redeemable within a month. For salaried workers, the debt was paid at *moon die*, the end of the month. For those of us hustlers, there was a limit beyond which no signing was done until the outstanding arrears was cleared. It was a good arrangement which compensated well for the tasteless food.

"Kay, I am done with the bucket, you can take your bath now."

My fellow street boys called me Kay, for Kojo. I dropped Nkrabeah the moment I left Moseaso, it roused too many bad memories.

There were two buckets used for bathing, and it was first-wake-first-use basis. I walked to the back of the building. It was still dark, so I had to walk carefully. Since we bathed in the open, we needed to rise a long while before the sun. I opened the tap and filled up the bucket with water. The owner of the store in front of which we slept provided the water as part of the rent. To ensure that only those who were paid up had access to the water, our headman (elected by us as his contact) had the key to the lock on the tap. Within minutes, I was done. The next person was waiting for the bucket.

Akwasi Poku brought the news. Akilipee was back from the big city and even his language and walking had changed. Kwame Nsuamoah was his real name. As long as we could remember, Nsuamoah had nurtured dreams of leaving Moseaso for the high life.

He wore baggy jeans, which were held in place with a belt the width of a crocodile matchet, and a buckle as huge as an orange, the shape of a mask. On the front of his big T-shirt, he had the inscription "Accra Boyz are Blezzed". On his feet, he had over-sized boots which we saw in the films shown in the Sadisco hotel and he had money to spend, lots!

"Nkrabeah, you have to come to the big city. I tell you, Moseaso is so dull! How do you guys even survive in this hell of a place?" He said the last sentence in the same way Mr. Brown, the white man who worked in the Adensu Mines, spoke.

I was impressed with the phrase *hell of a place*. It sounded sophisticated. Akwasi and I exchanged looks, he seemed impressed too.

We sat on the tree trunk which had been lying by the Ehyire river ever since we were young. The only time I could sneak from the house was in the afternoon, when I fetched water to fill the plastic barrels and pans. It was close to Christmas. Christmas was also the time for the Onum festival, which brought most of the indigenes of Moseaso back home to visit family and enjoy the peace and tranquility of the village.

"The big city has nice things we dreamt about when we were in school. Within one week of arriving there, I got a job in the factory of a white man called Mr. Darlington Griffiths."

The name of Akilipee's boss awed us as well. Akilipee had been away for two years. He said he was a driver in the factory. A driver in only two years! Whilst in the same period, I was slaving in Moseaso, not knowing what the future held for me. A plan began to form in my mind.

Opanyin Nemi was our local rich man. He had four trucks, called W'ato Nkyene, that left the village every morning to four destinations – Kumasi, Takoradi, Asankragwa and Enchi - and returned at night. You miss his trucks and you would have to walk to the main road, which was about five miles out. Getting a vehicle from there wasn't even assured. His trucks were recognised by the inscription in front and at the back, Time Changes and Dɛbi Asɛm, respectively.

My first hurdle was how to get out of the house without raising any suspicions. That was tough, because even though I wake up at 3 am to start sweeping, cleaning and scrubbing, I usually started my trips to the river around 5:30 am to fetch water. The W'ato Nkyene for Takoradi started loading at 4:30 am, and could be full quickly, especially on Mondays, the day I had selected. My second worry was how to avoid Opanyin Nemi. He didn't trust his drivers very much and usually went on trips with them, with his bag, to collect the fares himself. With his cars plying four routes, my prayer was that he would not be on the Takoradi route on the D-day. Being a good friend of my Wofa Akrumah, he was sure to enquire from me where I was going and to report back even if I convinced him with a lie. Worse case, he could turn me back home. I prayed for the first time in many years. I had written God off; there was no way He could be alive or a caring One, when He watched unconcerned whilst I suffered. Why did He not prevent my parents' demise?

Fate was favourable that day. Opanyin Akrumah's oldest sister, who lived in Ankosia, fell during a heavy downpour in her village and Wofa had to rush there the same dawn that I had planned to leave Moseaso. A week before D-day, I had sent a tiny bundle of my personal belongings to Poku's house and so it played into my plans so well when I had to accompany Opanyin Akrumah to the station for him [Opanyin Akrumah] to join the truck going to Kumasi. I smiled when I saw Mr. Nemi sitting infront of the truck; Wofa joined him. I said a silent prayer, God must be waking up now, I thought.

I didn't return home. Poku and I sat at the back of the truck, careful not to attract attention. Freedom beckoned, yet we bottled our excitement, fearful that it could easily be only a dream if anyone found out what we were doing. As the vehicle turned around the bend over the little bridge that crossed the stream behind the Omanhene's palace, under the bamboo trees under which we had played many games in happier times, away from Moseaso, towards Adaamaso and freedom, I took one last backward glance and held back a stray tear – my emotions were ambivalent.

Akilipee met us at the Neoplan Station in Circle, we got to Accra just as it was getting dark. Akilipee had told us how to get onto a Neoplan bus

in Takoradi; fortunately, the station in Takoradi wasn't far from the last stop for the Moseaso bus. It was a happy re-union, Poku and I beaming with smiles. We were in the promised land, finally.

We were overwhelmed by the size of Akili's house - it was even bigger than the Moseaso Omanhene's palace, which was the biggest mansion we had ever seen. The space in front of the mansion was about half the size of the RC Middle School 'A' school park. There were three big cars parked in the compound. When we entered the house, Poku turned to look at me. Our thoughts might have converged. Paradise existed on earth, in Ghana, and Akilipee was its annointed prophet. But we wondered whether the mansion was really for our friend. When we mustered courage and asked him, Akilipee hesitated for a split second before informing us that the house was for his boss, who had travelled out of the country, so he was taking care of it for awhile. We didn't care one bit - it was heaven.

Akilipee would usually spend the day with us and go for his night duties at the factory. For the first two weeks, we knew only bliss. Akilipee had all the films we used to watch at Sadisco, Opanyin Koduah's hotel. Snake in the Monkey's Shadow, I Trust my Leg, Shakkar, The Drunken Master, Bruce Lee, all our favorite Chinese and Indian films. We watched all of them again and more. We looked forward to Akilipee's return in the mornings; because we were eager to start work in the factory and our friend said he was working on it. Even though we were having a free time in his house, we didn't want to overstretch his benevolence. He insisted that he didn't mind.

I went over to join the queue at Sulley Maame's and was soon sitting on the bench, my waakye in a plastic bowl, interspersed with coloured gari and spagetti (popularly called taalia); a roll of wele and a small piece of fish completed the assembly. My shoe shine box sat safely by my feet, the working day had began for me.

When Akilipee told us that we were to start working the next day, we were excited. We hadn't come to Accra to watch the sea (which we were yet to see anyway); we wanted to get rich just as Akilipee, Poku and I having decided that Akilipee may be hiding his real wealth from us. We were to start on the evening shift as well, Akilipee informed us.

D-Day and we were ready by 7pm. We joined Akilipee in his Toyota Pickup, wearing the same overalls he wore for work. Dark blue overalls.

After my breakfast, I set off from the waakye spot, and took the road towards Maxwell Hotel. Turning right, I made it past Alewa's house. Alewa was my regular customer but he was away that week. I headed towards Ebony. An hour later, I had served only three people; it wasn't a good morning.

Akilipee told us we were going to see the Shift Supervisor for safety induction before we could begin work. Akilipee turned onto an untarred road and stopped in front of a shed by the roadside. About four men climbed onto the back of the pickup and a heavyset man appeared by the side of the car. He motioned us to get out. It was the Shift Supervisor.

I heard someone calling 'Shine, shine' and I turned. When I saw the person calling me, my heart missed a beat.

When we got out of the pickup truck, Poku and I exchanged glances. Is this the factory supervisor, we thought.

"Are these the new guys who are joining us, Scorpion?"

"Yes Boss," Akilipee responded.

Scorpion? Akilipee?

"Have you briefed them about today's operation?"

"No Boss, they only know they are starting the factory work today, on night shift."

"Good, let's get this shift started then!"

I immediately knew Poku and I were in trouble. We had been lured by Akilipee into robbery and this was to be our onboarding operation. We hit the first house, and when the fire exchange with the police began, the contents of my stomach got the relief they had been seeking since we first encountered the Boss. I also found my voice, and started screaming and running, and running...

I ended up days later on the street. I still can't recollect how I survived after escaping the crossfire. I didn't see Poku again, and was afraid that Akilipee and his gang would come looking for me. I lived in fear for months and tried to move away as far as possible from the house we hit on. Being a stranger in Accra meant I really didn't know where I was moving to. After months of moving from place to place, I settled in Alajo, sleeping in front of the shop. To survive, I learnt the art of shining shoes.

I knew I had drifted to a new territory that morning. When I saw the security man who had called for a shoe shine boy, I froze. A moment's hesitation and recognition dawned on both sides.

"You! You were one of them!"

He was the guy at the gate who had let us into that house we went to rob, as Akilipee had become friends with him a few weeks before the operation, as part of the modus operandi.

I turned, and ran, again.

I miss Moseaso. I have become a fugitive in this false promised land. I write these concluding words from the Neoplan station. I am returning to Moseaso. Our elders say that when the bow snaps, it goes back to its roots. I am returning to Moseaso. I know not what the future holds, but at least, I can stop running in Moseaso. My roots in Moseaso still remain a memento in my memory. I shall return to caress this memory and take it from there.

GUARDIAN OF
THE RENTED WELL

he man behind the desk was bent over sheets of paper spread all over the desk. He was seriously working, oblivious of the rhythmic humming of the air conditioner, the soft music being played on the radio and the continuous knocking on his door. The secretary, who was not unaware of this occasional eccentric behaviour of her boss, opened the door and entered the office after knocking for well over three minutes. The man still went on writing, his handsome face contorted in concentration.

Miss Ocansey smiled at the bent form of her boss. She really loved working with him; she had been with him for about three years as his personal assistant and she had loved every minute of it. What a boss to serve! Committed, dedicated – and handsome too.

Mr. Benson Stephen was a man of about thirty two years. Slim and tall, he had a body which spelt inner strength and a face bright with intelligence and vision. A graduate of Oxford University, he was the head of the publishing firm, Alonte & Associates, based in Ghana. A leading firm, it was noted for bestsellers in Africa and the plan for the future was to launch into the Caribbeans. Best known by the abbreviation AAA or 3A, Alonte & Associates' strength lay in unearthing new authors and making them stars. Some of the titles churned out in their six years of existence included House Matters, Turn Not a Blind Eye, Haunted Hunters and A Comedy of Saints.

Stephen was unmarried and a flirtatious bachelor of the highest degree. He held the enviable title of the most eligible bachelor in Accra.

****

Akos, aren't you leaving for home?"

"I will, soon. Just want to finish this plot I am working on for the second novel. I told you I finished the first novel and I'm presently looking for a publisher, right?"

"No, you didn't! You kept that from me! Congrats, my girl. Soon, I will be bragging that I know the best romantic writer in Sikaman."

"Haha, you are always building up grandiose images! Well, let's say amen to that!"

"Bye, my dear, do leave soon, OK?"

Akosua tried hard to balance her day job as an engineer with what she called her real job - writing. From an early age, she had dabbled in literary pursuits and her passion for that had never waned. At the end of each day, after rounding up her work as the production shift manager at Bombay Industries, where she oversaw the soaps production lines, she sat behind her desk, thinking, jotting, drafting and writing. It was her way of de-stressing, she just loved writing. Her friend Jemima was her biggest support. After seeing Jemi off halfway to the main gate, Akos returned to her desk and read, again, the last chapter of the manuscript of her first novel "The Showdown".

****

"Sir, a visitor to see you, please."

He still went on writing. Miss Ocansey hesitated for sometime, and tried again. This time, Mr. Benson looked up and realised for the first time that it was past mid-day and that he was very hungry. He had been working for about five continuous hours on the novel, *A day to Remember*, written by one of his best clients, Nii Noi Narh Snr., A great writer and novelist. He wanted to finish it within the month and take a well-deserved rest for a period of time.

"Yes, what can I do for you, Miss?"

"A lady visitor to see you, sir. Can I show her in?"

"Yes, yes. Please do and a cup of coffee for me, please." With that, he resumed his work, with the same serious concentration.

He looked up soon to meet the stare of a lovely lady, standing a short distance away from his desk. She was about twenty-five, he reasoned, and by God, beautiful. For a moment he stared absent-mindedly at her before he came to himself and showed her to a chair in front of him.

The lady sat down gracefully, and with the same flair placed her handbag on her lap. A split moment of silence as their eyes met…

"Mr. Benson Stephen at your service, ma'am."

He had said this a million and two times in his career and he always felt refreshingly confident each time. Today was no exception. It always assured him of his competence.

"Akosua Nketia is my name. I am an author. I have a novel I want published."

"A novel?"

"Yes. A friend recommended you highly to me at a party. She said you were the best this side of the world; so I decided to come over to see you. I have the manuscript here. Can you take a look, sir? Here, thank you."

A knock on the door, and the secretary entered with the steaming cup of coffee. Miss Nketia politely refused Mr. Benson's offer to have a cup made for her. He took the manuscript and skimmed it, taking sips of the coffee intermittently. Having finished with the script, he placed it on the desk and smiled at the lady.

"Can I call you Akos? Good. The work is perfect, the plot is excellent, I am just in love with the suspense and your climax is just splendid. I think you've got a deal. Anyway, everyone will like to deal with a … beautiful lady like you."

Adroit at fending off the attentions of men, Akosua answered: "I am glad to hear that, Mr. Stephen..."

"No, no, no, you gave me permission to call you Akos; please call me Ben."

"...does that mean you will publish it?" She wanted to be sure she heard well, trying very hard to contain her excitement.

"My dear Akos, I said you got a deal. Well… let's see…can you meet me on Friday at eh…Sadisco Hotel so we can discuss this in more detail? At 4.00 pm? Good. See you then."

****

His major challenge when he heard that he was to spend six months in Kigali was how his sweetheart would fare in his absence. They had been together for close to six years, and their childlessness had even made brought them closer – a couple united against their two families, who in their earnestness and anxiety pestered them each day with questions and suggestions – to see one odifuo or medicine man or the other.

His closest pal, Kofi Adaboh, was excited, however, to be away from his wife. Kofi was the most adventurous person he had ever known, and his expectation was that Kigali would offer both danger and exploration, exploration amongst the natural delights of a foreign land.

****

"Akos, tell me, what do you do with your beauty?"

Benson hated to beat the side of the drum when the top was available.

"Is that how you flatter all your female clients?"
"No, only the special and pretty ones."
"I see...."

She smiled shyly and sipped her beer.

Across from Sadisco, the traffic was beginning to build into the evening rush hour, time for workers to drive home, for trotro mates to bluff the passengers they begged for during mid-day, for the sun to begin setting. Akos remembered the days she spent during her childhood with her grandmother; in the village, where the setting of the sun was glorious. In Accra, no one paid attention to it, traffic made nonsense of every other consideration.

Benson watched her pensive face, her countenance reflecting the glow he felt sitting with her; a new fish in his pond. He couldn't wait to start fishing.

****

A man thinks he chases a woman, to win her; but a careful observer of the oldest game in life knows that a man chases a woman until she catches him. Benson's wooing of Akosua was relentless, focused and determined. Akosua's evasiveness made her even more desirable.

When after two months of fast-track work on her novel, Benson called Akosua on a Friday to tell her "The Showdown" could hit the press in a matter of weeks, she couldn't refuse his offer of a celebratory dinner at Sadisco. This time, she couldn't suppress the exhilaration in her voice.

The night turned out to be a long one, with a lot of dancing together. At midnight when they parted, both had no doubt in their minds that they were in for something more than a business relationship.

"Friday nite" turned out to be a favourite time for the two of them. They went out together to many places, and were hardly apart. Akosua ended up partly giving up her house, and staying with Stephen. This, of course, had a great effect on Stephen's commitment to his work, failing to publish Nii Noi Narh's novel, and even that of Akosua; actually, she didn't care for it any longer. They continued this relationship with an intensity akin to madness.

****

Lt. Patrick Atiemo had returned from Rwanda to find his marital home empty, his wife nowhere to be found. He wanted to surprise her, so he didn't send any notice of his arrival date. The next day when she did not return from wherever he presumed she had travelled to, he called on a good friend of his to enquire about Akos, as he was getting worried. What his friend told him shook him to his very bones. His wife going out with someone and, not just that, sleeping in his house as well. He just couldn't take it.

What Akosua didn't tell Benson was that she was married to Lieutenant Patrick Atiemo, and that her husband was on a peace-keeping mission in Rwanda.

Back home, Patrick thought about the whole situation. He wasn't one given to wine but he drank that day, tears streaming down his face like a waterfall. All these years he had lived for his wife alone, toiled to make her life comfortable, been faithful to her. In Rwanda, whilst his colleagues sampled the native women, he had remained faithful to his vows, to love Akos and only her. And what does she offer in return? God, he surely had to end it all. End it, blast it, shoot the bastards in their stomachs for sure.

He took out his pistol and loaded it. His military mind was set in motion. They were the enemy. He knew what he had in mind, the enemy didn't. He knew they existed, they didn't. His next move was to find them.

Benson and Akosua had had a wonderful day. Akos had finally agreed, after a lot of persuasion, to take him to her house. In high spirits, they entered the sitting room. Stephen instantly felt Akos freeze beside him at the sight of the man sitting behind the dining table with the pistol in his hand. Akos just couldn't believe her eyes. She never expected her husband to be back so soon; at least, he should have written to inform her he was coming home.

Before she could recover from her shock, two shots rang out – a bullet each finding its mark in Akos and Stephen. As they fell, Atiemo shot his head off.

Benson was shocked the most about the whole incident. As he went down in pain, he cried "Oh God, save me…" but all he could perceive was darkness, deep darkness enveloping him…

He was almost certain he was in heaven, and an angel was looking down at him. All around him was bright light. This must be the light that, he learnt ages ago in Sunday school, was supposed to shine forth from the throne of God.

The angels moved about. All he could whisper was "Have mercy, Lord, and give me another chance, another chance."

Slowly, his gaze focused and the haziness cleared. He was looking up at a nurse, and he realised that he was not in heaven but in a hospital, and the nurse holding his hand was speaking to him.

"Yes, He will give you a chance again, sir. Thank God you are alive and recovering. Been in a coma for the past three days. Shot in the shoulder, you were the only one alive out of the three. You must occupy a special place in God's heart."

****

He mounted the pulpit and as he sang "He holds my life" with the congregation, he bowed his head to say a prayer. Today, he was going to preach to the youth fellowship and young couples, to keep faith with the wives of their youth, to drink from their own cistern. He felt moved to make it a personal sermon, to share his experience as a guardian of a rented well, and how he nearly lost his life at the hands of the owner of that well.

FACE TO FACE –
TROTRO PALAVER

The engineer who designed the bus would have surely been surprised to find that one of his handiworks was still on the road, so many years after the assembly plant had been decommissioned. There was the likelihood that he might not even recognize it as one of those that left his factory. A new guy at Kokompe had left his mark on the old Morris bus. The *troski*, as all the locals called their regular passenger vehicles, carried registration number ABC 4037.

"Lagos Town, New Town, Circle! Lagos Town, New Town, Circle, ready going!" Akwasi shouted, calling out in all directions, his brownish towel on his shoulder, already soaked with sweat in the 30 degree centigrade sun. Intermittently, he would wring it to squeeze out the sweat.

"Yeessssss", almost singing the drawn-out word. "Ready going. Only two more to go, come, are you going?" Akwasi crossed the street to help a lady who ended up going to another vehicle; she was headed for Maamobi rather.

Even though there were six people seated in the trotro, only one of them was a real passenger. The rest were mates and drivers in the Abedi station. Sitting in the bus was a ploy to encourage commuters to join the bus, thinking that it was almost full.

Abedi station was situated in the Pig Farm area, the area's name dating back to the days when a nearby joint was the best place in Accra to get domedo, fried and spiced pork. It was a pork factory. Lines of frying pots could be found at the joint and one could get the domedo hot, spiced, with accompaniment of ringed onions and pepper powder. The station was managed by the Ghana Private Road Transport Union (GPRTU), an affiliate of the Trades Union Congress. Some called the union *Gepretu of Tuk*. The executives were usually retired, old drivers. Efo Gayon was the station master.

"Yessssss, Circle, New Town, Kokomlemle, Lagos Town, air-conditioned bus, away bus, ready going!" There were twelve people now, and the other mates and drivers gave each other cues to begin getting off strategically as the bus filled up.

The vehicle was actually a lorry which had been converted into a passenger bus. The capacity was written as part of the particulars of the bus on the driver's door: nineteen, which included the driver. In the lingua of the station, the sitting arrangements were distributed sixteen back, two front. The driver's seat was not included in the tally.

The driver was separated from the main compartment behind him by a wire mesh. This compartment contained two wooden benches, arranged parallel to each other such that when the passengers sat, they faced each other. Even though the driver's mate admitted sixteen passengers to occupy the benches, he would insist on sitting as well.

"Master Kojo! Master! The car is almost full, we can go now."

The driver walked slowly to the bus, a toothpick busy in his mouth; he was using it like a ceiling brush to remove scattered cobwebs of meat stuck in his teeth. He had just completed a meal of *fufu* and *akrantie,* a specialty of Daavi Ama, who had been operating her chop bar in the station for decades.

"Mate, we are seven on each bench already. Is it not full? Are you going to sit yourself?"
"No, we are not full. It is one-man-one-seat, eight on each bench."

"Ah *mate yi paa*, what one-man-one-seat? Do you understand what that means? Hahaha!"

The other passengers joined in the laughter. Soon, a new passenger joined the bench behind the driver.

"Mate," the latest passenger, a man dressed in factory overalls, enquired, "there is no more space on this bench. How can I fit?"

Akwasi ignored him and called out for one more passenger.

"Mate, are you not going to answer my question?" The factory guy shouted. "And where are you going to sit, won't you sit on the last available space on this other bench?"
"Ask and ask again, massa," the lady who had asked Akwasi the same question earlier on interjected, "I asked him the same question and he told me this rickety bus of his is one-man-one-seat!"

A lady who was clearly in a hurry came running and was grateful when Akwasi asked her to sit on the little space he indicated on the bench.

With the touching of wires, the driver got the engine running. At the cue of 'Away bus' from Akwasi, Master Kojo took off and then applied his brakes suddenly, as if on cue! The dilemma of inadequate space on the benches was solved immediately, as each passenger was thrown in the direction of the driver and the packing was completed!

Akwasi squeezed himself by the last lady to join the bus, half sitting, half perching, with the door slightly opened.

"Mate, I will alight at Robert Motors, how much will that be?"

"Madam, that will be the same fare as if you were going to Abavanna Junction."

"What! Driver!"

"Akwasi, what is the matter back there?"

In *troskis*, it was usual for the driver to communicate through his mate, like a chief via his linguist.

"Master, it is this madam here who doesn't want to pay the fare!"

"Hey mate, did I say I won't pay? I just questioned the fare from Pig Farm to Robert Motors. Just a stone throw, I could even have walked!"

"Akwasi, charge her the fare for Abavanna Junction!"

It wasn't a happy lady who alighted at Robert Motors, a mechanical shop. So when Akwasi told her he didn't have exact change for her, she blew her top. Another passenger, a mechanic, also alighted at the same spot, so Akwasi gave them a combined change to divide between them.

"Hey, small boy, where do I know this man from? Is he my brother or husband? If you don't give me my change now, you will smell pepper!"

****

"Why do people chew garlic at all?"

"Adɛn, Auntie, why do you ask that question?"

The lady who asked the initial question tried hard not to look straight ahead, and the gentleman who sat directly opposite her on the other bench also avoided her gaze, electing to concentrate on the front of the bus.

"My brother, poverty is expensive o. Otherwise, why would one have to endure all sorts of smells in this enclosure of a bus?"

"Baaaaaaas stop! Abavanna!"

When the 'garlic' man got down, everyone exhaled audibly. Apparently, everyone knew why the lady asked the question about garlic. Typical of Ghanaians, everybody knew what was on everybody's mind, yet when the question was posed, a question was asked to clarify.

At Abavanna, Master Kojo realized that most of his colleague drivers were joining the Nkansa-Djan-Pig Farm road from the road coming from the Maamobi Polyclinic, instead of the usual route from the Kotobabi Police Station. He got suspicious, and guessed that the police were at it again at the Catholic church junction.

He took off and turned right, towards Abavanna down, via Waist and Power junction.

"Yes, front...froooont, please."

There were two passengers sitting in the front cabin and one of them, a lady, passed her fare through the wire mesh. The note was passed along to the mate. The second passenger turned to look at the driver, who kept his eyes dogged on the road ahead.

"Massa...yes, you in front, your fare please!"
"Mate, my change, before I forget it." That was the lady in front.
Her change was exactly the amount the man in front needed to pay. Driver's mates were experts at what was termed Kweku Ananse

mathematics, substitution by shifting around.

"Madam, please collect your change from the man sitting by you, it is exactly the amount I need to give you."

The driver still didn't turn to the passengers' direction at all. The male passenger in front started fidgeting - that was not how things were to happen: the driver was his neighbour at Kotobabi Down and he expected him to exempt him from paying the trotro fare.

Immediately after the male passenger gave his fare to the lady, the trotro went past the SWAG park and turned right towards the K1 and 2 schools and, for the first time, the driver acknowledged his neighbour's presence in the car.

"Ei, Opia, is that you? I didn't notice you had joined koraa o."

Apuuu, wicked man, thought Opia. See his face like a goat! Azaa man!

The troski went past Honesty, so named because the owner of Honesty Transport used to live at that junction, his articulated trucks marked 'Honesty'. Whether or not it reflected his personal philosophy was another matter.

Past the Providence School signpost, Master Kojo stopped at K1&2 for a passenger to alight. At Prempeh hotel, a new passenger joined the troski. Whilst waiting for the passenger to settle, Massa Kojo flagged one of his colleague drivers.

"Dovlo, are they there?" It was obvious to the other driver who 'they' referred to.

"Yes o, ma broda. At the Catholic church junction, just around the corner from Agbajena. They dey there. Today, they are collecting twice the normal rate. Atta Papa just got charged for not having a torchlight in his bus, this hot afternoon!"

"*Ewurade medaase*! I could smell them from Abavanna!"

****

"Please, can you pass your money from the left? Please don't give me big notes."
"Why shouldn't we? Shouldn't you have coins for change?"
"Madam, I think it is just a polite request from the boy. Please allow small."

"Mate, I will drop at the Catholic church junction."

It was a sleepy voice; the passenger, an elderly man, had gone to sleep as soon as he boarded the troski at Abedi station.

"Oh Papa, we didn't pass there o. We are now at Nkansa-Djan."
"Ah, why didn't you pass there?"
"Papa, I asked at Abavanna whether anyone would get down at Roman, but there was no response."
"It was because he was busily snoring and hitting people's shoulders with his head!" The lady who sat on the old man's right didn't sound amused. The other passengers laughed.
"Driver, please turn the car, I have to get down at Roman. Driver!"
"Akwasi!"
"Master!"
"*Wetin* again? *Asem ben*?"

"Master, is it not this man? He has been sleeping aah, now that we have passed his stop, he wants us to take him back."

"Opanyin," Massa Kojo tried to be polite "you know we can't take you back, not in this traffic, even if I want to do it. I will let you get down right here. Akwasi, open the door for him. Papa, next time, please stay alert."

"Ah, but I need some balance to take a new troski back to the Catholic church junction."

"But you have not even paid me!"

"I paid you!"

"Ei, you this man, you have been sleeping throughout this trip, when did you pay me?"

It quickly became obvious that the old man didn't have money on him. A good Samaritan paid for him. When he insisted that he be given money to take a bus back to his original destination, all the passengers broke down in mirth and called him Papa Oliver. The good Samaritan had to come to his aid, again.

****

"Mate, why should I pay the full fare to Circle? I am using only half of my allocated space on this bench!"

The speaker was seated by a plump lady; she looked like a Makola Market woman who was on her way to the market. Her load of dried fish in a basket was placed under one of the benches.

"Owula, are you referring to me?"

"Mate, I say I will not pay the full fare! Take the balance from wherever

you deem fit!"

"My view is that some people should pay double the fare, for the space they actually occupy, otherwise they cheat some of us." That was Opia, who had recovered from his anger to contribute to the discussion in the troski.

"True. It is supposed to be one-man-one-seat, but for some, it is one-man-two seats!"

The Makola woman kept her cool; only a foolish dog will run after a flying bird and this was a topic she wouldn't win.

"Lagos Town *wo mu o,* mate!"

At Lagos Town, Massa Kojo got down to open the bonnet of the Morris troski. A steam of vapor exuded from the engine, and the driver had to step back, almost jumping. Akwasi knew what to do, retrieving a 5 liter gallon from under his bench and crossing the road to get some water.

"Driver, what is wrong? We are in a hurry o!"

"Oh, nothing is wrong!"

"How can it be 'nothing' when we have been here for almost five minutes?"

"It is small 'overheating', we have to let the engine cool down, it is normal."

"Mate! Please give me my balance, I can't wait, I have an appointment I can't miss."

"Oh *bra,* wait small, we will finish *noor,* and we will be going."

Soon it was obvious that the problem was more than engine overheating. Massa Kojo took a mat from under his seat and spread it under the car, vanishing under the car. The passengers could hear some hammering.

"Ei Driver! If the car cannot move again, give us our money *la!*"

Massa Kojo didn't respond. He went back to the front of the car, poured in some more water, and climbed back into his seat. After the third attempt, the troski came to life, and the journey could continue.

"Hey, buddy", shouted another passenger. "Keep your dir-rry hands off ma suit! You gat me?" All in something resembling an American twang. It's what everyone has now come to call LAFA – locally acquired foreign accent.
"Massa, watch how you talk to me! Who do you think you are?"
"Who do I think I am? Do you know who I am? You fitters just get out of your workshop and come and sit in cars, can't you change your overalls if you are going out?"
"I agree with you, boss. Hey fitter, see how dirty your coat is. Do you want to soil the man's nice attire?"
"Did I not pay the same fare?" That was the mechanic. "If he thinks he is a big man, he should buy his own car and ride in it!"

"Baaaasssss stop! Mate, I will *drop* at Malata!"

When the man in suit got down, Akwasi spoke what was on his mind. "Eish, these myself people! *Nsem piii!*"

From Malata through Kokomlemle to Circle, the journey was smooth. Almost. The fitter's attire was the main discussion point, and he agreed that indeed he needed to have a spare attire to wear when leaving the workshop to buy spare parts. He was on his way to Abossey Okai.

Just before the station at Circle, around Odo Rise, the Morris troski came to an abrupt halt. *Aponkye brake.*

Reason? The fuel had run out. Finito.
With one voice, the passengers chorused "One gallon!"

Fortunately, the last stop, the Kwame Nkrumah Circle station, was a walking distance and as they alighted, Akwasi retrieved another gallon. He knew what to do.

PROJECT AKOMA

He was pleased with himself for making it early to the classroom. The morning was good and the milieu, silent. It had rained the previous day, so the air blew humidly into the classroom, turning the peaceful ambience into soothing balm. For the umpteenth time that morning he was grateful to be alive.

He was alone and the lecture would not begin for a half hour yet. This was a good time to think about Adjoa, the second year beauty on Continental Block. It was time to reflect, to take stock, and then to re-strategize how to win that lovely girl's love.

The heart decides, but it is the mind that plans. His heart had decided to love Adjoa two semesters ago. His nerves, couriers for his heart, sent the message marked "Urgent" to his busy brain. It simply read: "I have found my desire—my missing rib," and set his brain in motion.

It had seemed impossible. Adjoa was hard to get—a quintessential "no-go-area." What is worse, she lived on the last floor of Continental Block, where male visitors are prone to surveillance from the lodge of her uncompromising Hall Tutor. That is not all. She was already in her second year and he a mere freshman. She took her classes in the Faculty of Arts, but all of his were in the Science Faculty. How would they find common ground to meet?

When the heart decides and the mind is in motion a course is set to reach its fruition, finding avenues, exploiting ways and creating means. Thus, Project Heart was born. He recruited friends to form a team: to review extant knowledge on the object of his interest, to consider the best methodologies for securing her heart and to estimate potential gains against his likely costs.

Project Heart recommended an expensive gift. It seemed a good start because it won him her time, and the more gifts he brought won more time with her——a visit this week, two the next, then three and more. Her roommates' attitudes were encouraging and her reception wasn't bad, she even offered to see him off——he jumped at the chance for a quiet night's stroll—everything seemed perfect and according to plan.

Project Heart said it was time to spill the beans. The moment seemed golden. The stars were in the sky. Night birds tweeted him luck. Crickets chirruped a moonlight serenade. Shrubs danced around them like cherubs in the night. And when she stopped and said, "I have to go to my hall now, this is how far I can bring you," he held her hand and let out, "I love you."

The whole world must have stopped to listen: the night birds, the cherub-like shrubs, the crickets, moon and the stars; all the members of Project Heart, ears intent hiding in the shadows; his heart, his brain and the nerves that had engaged them in this mission. All waited an eternity of the second before she said . . .

"No, we can only be friends"

The mind makes the plans but when it fails it is the heart that hurts. His heart had lived the hurt but it still dreamed of living its hope, and if there was any sign of hope it was in the soothing solace of the classroom in which he sat, in the refreshing air the rain had cleansed, and in the simple fact of being alive for which he still felt grateful. He had loved and lost and lived to love again. Someday there might just be another Project Heart.

Made in the USA
Columbia, SC
19 December 2018